Light the Way

S. COURTNEY

FOREWORD

1

ELIVIA

"Now, over your shoulder with a bit more pout, good. Look slightly down and to your right. There! DON'T MOVE!"

Click click click click click

"Okay, now give me seductive, alluring. Yes, sexy Mrs. Claus, you'll melt the North Pole in that red lace garter and those heels that scream 'take me'!"

I giggled, "Sven, darlin', they're called fuck me heels... for a good reason." I should know as I proudly hold up my cherry red six-inch stilettos. Everyone's laughing at my explicit humor, but Sven looks horrified. He frowns, "Such filthy language should not leave those perfectly pouted lips."

Right, because pretty girls aren't supposed to curse.

Whatever.

Everyone I ever worked with is here to witness my final photoshoot. It's a double issue: A Winter Wonderland spread to send me off in style. It's my favorite time of year, and what better way than to give me my dream theme? We showcased all the best in holiday wear from sexy Mrs. Claus, the gorgeous Grinch, a naughty elf, and a red-hot Rudolph, complete with a cherry red nose and matching thong. Every Christmas fantasy your heart could ever desire. This shoot lasted three days, ending today with the most dramatic look, the Ice Queen lingerie. Think Frosty the Snowman's sexy young wife.

I'm ready to say goodbye, finally! I'm over this fast-paced lifestyle, commuting from Garden City into metro New York in four-inch heels. I wake up at 5 a.m. to barely get to the office by 7:30 a.m. and work well after the sun goes down.

I could have lived within city limits, but the thought of seven roommates in a tiny efficiency apartment. No way. Plus, the bathroom would be down the hall. You've heard the nightmare stories about filthy communal bathrooms.

In Garden City, it feels like a noise barrier was placed around the city. I love the peace and tranquility of my apartment. I can hear birds chirping and the water running from a nearby tributary.

It was a decent place for a small-time model for Sugar Sweet Lingerie, where *'He'll buy ANYTHING to taste your honey pot.'* As corny as it sounds, our quarterly catalog has two million subscribers and over 70 brick-and-mortar stores. Not bad for a company starting from the ground up, not backed by big-name corporations. No, they began with four local sponsors and now have over 100 international companies who love having their products in our magazine.

But alas, my time is over; I gave them six years, and now I'm too old.

I'm 28, by the way.

In this industry, 25 is over the hill. I might as well set my dentures in a glass of Alka seltzer at the door and put on my warming shawl while knitting and watching Golden Girls.

I have a meeting with my boss to discuss the next steps. I want to hone my managerial skills in a new location. They're constantly expanding, and I know they have a few stores opening up soon, right before Christmas; maybe I'll help there.

"All right, my holiday beauty, I need you on the XXX pleasure pillow with the icy blue lace set. Makeup, it's time for the Ice Queen look! Everyone else reconvene in an hour and a half." I sashay toward the dressing room to change into outfit #8 and the most detailed look.

~

Nick

I'VE BARELY HEARD the Chief talking about the upcoming holiday volunteer duties. My focus is on the town's prestigious holiday decorating contest. My mom and dad participated and made it a family tradition for as long as I can remember. There was a period where they won six years in a row until my dad passed away suddenly, and not even a week later, my mom joined him. It's the saddest, sweetest love story I've ever witnessed.

When mom was in the hospital, she told me to compete to remind me of the good times, but my heart couldn't take it. Every year, walking around and seeing the beautiful displays shattered me. I found myself reminiscing about seeing my mom stare lovingly at my dad while she held the ladder as he strung up the lights.

I'm determined to win it to honor them and their eternal love. I will place it on the mantle next to their wedding photo and a funny picture they took in their ugliest holiday sweaters. Christmas meant a lot to my family, and I will continue the tradition as their only child. I see myself continuing this with my family in the future.

If I ever find someone.

Someone who wasn't a lying, manipulative, cheating wh...

"NICOLAS!"

"Huh?! Sorry, Chief."

"No need to apologize. You just volunteered as Santa for the company party and our week at the shopping center. Congratulations."

"But Chief, I got the annual holiday lights competition. I need all my free time to plan and execute."

"You'll have plenty of time. That's all, dismissed!"

I groan, not being able to plead my case. I shuffle over to my locker as my buddy checks the gauges on his oxygen tank and buttons up his supplies.

"Hey, hot Santa, are you ready to be groped and fondled by every woman in town?"

"It's not a bad deal unless one of my exes shows up. There's a good chance Kendra could after having baby number five. Safe to say, I dodged a bullet. Besides, it's better than being one of the reindeer or, worse, one of the elves in that dorky suit and elf shoes. I'll be eye candy. I might even snag a date or two. So, what's your holiday assignment?"

He scratches the back of his neck, "Umm, I'm one of your dorky elf helpers. Chief even named me…" He was hesitating; it couldn't be that bad, could it?

"I'm Jingles McSnowflake."

I couldn't stop the freight train of laughter roaring forward. It was from deep within. I tried my damndest to stop, but the name sounded like, "Jingle my snowflake!"

This is definitely revenge from when Beckham pranked him by stretching plastic wrap across the Chief's office door and covering it in shaving cream. Beckham rang the alarm, and Captain rushed out, hit the plastic wrap, slipped on the shaving cream, and the momentum caused him to end up on his ass. We ended up in a power drill session where he repeated that this was a 'one team, one fight' punishment but that this wouldn't be Beckham's only punishment. I guess he was right.

I wipe the tears from my eyes. Beckham was not amused, but I could also see the uptick in the corners of his mouth.

"Okay, you've laughed long enough. You're a terrible friend."

I'm trying to talk through the laughter, "And you know we have to take the station holiday photo. It'll hang proudly in the hallway; you'll never live it down!"

He smacks his forehead, "Fuck...I forgot! Kelly's going to laugh like you did when she hears this. Ooh, it's time for me to head home to see my girl. Four days without her feels like a month. Don't call me for at least 24 hours. I'll be busy." He smirks, and I wave him off, trying to get that image out of my head as I begin my five days on-call at the station house.

Sometimes, we do a 5/2 split week or the more common 4/3 split. I take the larger chunk because I'm single. It lets married and committed men get time with their families. I pull my blanket and pillow from my locker and throw them on the bed, plopping down to hatch my plan. No one would take this victory from me. I hope it stays quiet, at least for tonight.

2

ELIVIA

Knock knock*

*   "Come in, Elivia." I walk in and sit in front of his desk, slowly crossing my legs, exaggerating the motion before he shakes his head to focus. "Hey, Danny. The final shoot went well, so now you can put me in the old models' home for washed-up centerfolds."

Another quick glimpse, "Ohhh, you are more than a pair of gorgeous legs." I shifted them a bit, causing him to jolt out of whatever fantasy he and my legs were in. "Right. So, tell me, where am I going? I want my quiet home with the white picket fence."

"Yes, I remember. My dear, you will be relocated to Asher Falls in northwest Pennsylvania. The boutique-style store is located in a shopping center, and you'll be working with the sales associate on all aspects, including advertising, window display, and inventory. Are you really ready to give up the fast-paced life?"

"More than ready. I've always been in the middle of a huge, bustling metropolis. First Chicago, now New York. I love those Hallmark Christmas movies with the beautifully snow-blanketed town, festive with decorations everywhere. I'm hopeful for a happy-ever-after holiday. This will be my first opportunity to decorate a real home for Christmas. I will have a 6-foot-tall Douglas fir instead of my 3-foot plastic sham of a tree. I'm so excited! I mean, I'm excited about the job opportunity, too."

"I'm sure. Call the moving company and put it on our account when you're packed and ready to go. Good luck there and thank you for all you've given us here."

I shake Danny's hand, "It was my pleasure. I hope I blend in at Asher Falls." He shrugs his shoulders, and I get what he's implying. To blend in, I'll have to do something drastic. I can easily say goodbye to this long, straight boring hair and opt for beach waves: new town, new me.

I'm ready to leave all this behind, the pollution-filled air, the stuffy, packed nightclubs, and especially the arrogant, pretentious douchebags. I wouldn't tell Danny, but I wanted to fall in love like in those holiday movies. Surrounded by delicate snow flurries as he hoists me up and spins me around after I said yes to spending my life with him.

But first, I had to find my dream home in my tiny mountain town.

Nick

THANK ST. Florian, the patron saint of firefighters; my shift was pretty quiet. There were only a few calls, including an electrical fire at Mr. Swenson's shed because he was testing out his 47-year-old lights. He sustained moderate damage. We decided to confiscate the vintage hazards to avoid a future inferno. He was gearing up for the lights festival like everyone else in town.

When my parents died, I angrily tossed all holiday-related materials in heartbroken rage. I didn't understand what I did to deserve it. In retrospect, I should have stashed the decorations in the attic. I can replicate some of Mom's favorites and, at the same time, create new memories. I put my bunk stuff back in my locker and headed home.

When I pulled into my driveway, I noticed the 'for sale' sign next door had a big red 'sold' across it.

Oh, joy, new neighbors.

I turn on the news when I get inside, hoping to catch a promising snow forecast. Although it would make outside setup difficult, I've always loved the first blanket of snow. I sat for a moment to watch Lee Cunningham's report.

"Well, folks, we're getting close to optimal conditions for a winter wonderland. I predict a snowstorm in the next three weeks, and we should have a white Christmas for the Annual Holiday Lights competition. The official countdown starts now and good luck to everyone entering the steep competition."

After eating, I cleared all the forward-facing windows. Maybe this week, I'd clean the outside of my white two-story colonial with red shutters and matching door. You'd assume a traditional family lived here from the outside, but only one man is in this four-bedroom, three-bath home. It reminds me of my parent's house, and it's comforting. Besides, it has room to grow when it's time.

After a few more deliveries over the next few days, I'm ready to show my neighbors how serious I am.

Elivia

I FOUND the cutest mid-size cottage-style home! Although made primarily of brick and not wood, it is still cozy and comfy. It even has a traditional wood-burning fireplace! I can't wait to make it a boho-style paradise but, most importantly, show off my Christmas decorating skills. I may be the new girl, but I have a small-town heart. I'm so excited I scheduled the move immediately after I closed on the house.

"Thank you, Kelly, for working around the clock for this to happen so quickly. I'm super excited!"

"Of course, you're ready to live quietly amongst the trees."

"Something like that. It's my version of settling down...well, without the man and children part."

"Do you see that in your future?"

"As long as he's not hung up on what I used to do as a lingerie model, I'd love that. Let's keep that little tidbit between us. And to help separate from my former profession, I'm going to the salon for a new look. I'd like to be incognito since I'll work at the boutique. The only people who might recognize me are the men who come with their wives or girlfriends. And I highly doubt they'll say anything. Could you imagine?" We burst out laughing. I look down at my watch. "Got to run. When you're available, let's have lunch in town. Maybe you can tell me where to find a decent guy."

"Totally! We have a nice selection of attractive singles. A few officers, EMTs... Oh! The barista at the coffee shop is a hottie. I got lucky with a firefighter to call my husband."

"Sounds promising. Well, I'll let you know when I arrive. See you soon!"

As soon as I hung up, I was on the metro and seven stops later at Nancy's salon with only minutes to spare.

"Elivia! Cutting it close." She greets me sarcastically, knowing my hectic schedule.

I sat down, "Sorry, I was talking to my realtor. Wrapping up last-minute details." She runs her fingers through my hair, fluffing and shaking it around.

"So, you're really leaving, huh? You've been saying this since you came here and became a supermodel."

"I am not a..."

"Hey, I knew I recognized you!" A guy in the waiting area with the catalog in his hand interrupts us. Nancy made sure her shop was one of our subscribers.

"You're her!" He shows me the freshly printed issue of me in the sexy Mrs. Claus nightie, holding a plate of cookies and a glass of milk. He has the widest smile. "Because of you, I'm ordering this outfit for my girl. She's over there under the dryer."

Of course, she is. You wouldn't approach otherwise.

"So, can...could I get your autograph?" He produces a pen from seemingly out of nowhere.

You just happened to have a pen? Okay.

I signed it without a word and smiled. I sigh loudly as Nancy spins me to face the mirror, "Time to say hello to a new me. Shorten, highlight, and give me sexy beach waves, Nancy. I'm so ready!"

Eight days later, with a couple of boxes and an overnight bag, I'm on Highway 280 in my black with peanut butter interior Lexus ES. The drive was peaceful, with periods of snow-blanketed forests, hills, and mountains. I stopped a couple of times to be in awe of these picturesque views.

I hit the city limit around 9 p.m. Kelly said she'd leave the key in the mailbox. When I exited my car, it was much colder than New York, as I was north of the Susquehannock State Forest. The neighborhood was quiet and had a few streetlights to illuminate enough of the area not to look like a horror film. I look around and am in awe of how beautiful the houses look. I saw some starting to put up their lights; it was beginning to look festive. I ordered my decorations, which should arrive with my belongings or the next day, weather permitting. I yawn and feel the exhaustion of the long drive hit me like a ton of bricks. I grab my air mattress and overnight bag. Everything else can wait.

Despite being exhausted, I'm up at 5 a.m., as usual. I moved the remainder of my stuff from the car inside, at 7 a.m. I was dressed in a cozy cream and black checkered knit sweater dress and tan riding boots, ready to find the grocery store. Because it's such a small town, all the shops were centralized within a few blocks' radius. Maps said it was a five-minute drive. Before going further to the Asher Falls Market, I peeked at the shopping center where my new job would be.

Judging by the stares at the grocery store, it's safe to say they know there's a new girl in town. I smile and say hello as I peruse the aisles for only a few items to get me through the week. I'd do the extensive shopping once I was settled in. The cashier is trying to scan and stare at the same time. He fumbles a few times but eventually gets the food bagged. "Will that be all, ma'am?"

"Yes, thank you, Devon."

"You must be new in town. I've never seen someone so pretty." His eyes went wide. I don't think he was supposed to say that part out loud. He's adorable.

"Well, thank you. Yes, I got in last night." He takes my bags and follows me to my car, placing them in the trunk. I tip him and head back home. The movers should be here any moment.

3

NICK

I finished another shift at the station. It was a busy one, three medical emergencies, a call to the woods for an unauthorized bonfire, and a dumpster fire at the high school, damn kids. I thought I could sleep all day, but I couldn't due to all the beeping, clanging, and banging outside.

On my day off, of course.

All my current neighbors are usually considerate about my shift work, but of course, not the new guy.

That's strike one, buddy.

I growl out my frustration while getting up. Everything's sore, and everything hurts. I didn't bother to put on more than the boxers I had on.

I needed coffee...and a chiropractor.

When I round the kitchen, I have to shield my eyes against the sun. It was sitting outside the windows like a 10,000-watt searchlight. I yawn as I try to see the action happening next door from the dining room window while starting the pot. It was a small moving truck for a home that size. I spot a nice Lexus parked out front, but it doesn't give me much context on my rambunctious neighbor. Such a small truck shouldn't take too long to unload—perhaps another bachelor to hang out with.

Unless he's a douchebag.

I head upstairs with my coffee to layer up; it's downright frigid outside. I glanced out my bedroom window that faces the new neighbors. I watched the movers form a receiving line to put the boxes into the house. After bundling up, I finally go outside to the garage and take the snowmen two by two.

Crash

"What the hell?! Are you kidding me?! Those are platinum $2300 Chateau Baccarat crystal wine glasses!"

My ears perk up. That is definitely not a man. I see a dirty blonde in a cream-colored dress and knee-high boots leaning against the door. She hugged herself for warmth and frustratingly voiced her concern about how they handled her stuff. She huffed, throwing up her hands before stepping back inside. From her casual stance but sexy attire, I concluded she had to be married. No one like her ever moves here alone. Plus, $2300 wine glasses? Her husband must be one of those six-figure executives. I can pack away that seven-second fantasy I just had. I was still curious about who she was. Plus, it's rude if you don't welcome your new neighbors.

After dinner, I packed my bag for another shift in a couple of days—first, my snack bag, then my uniforms and basics upstairs. I came out with my travel toiletry bag in one hand while brushing my teeth with the other. I chuck it in my backpack before glancing outside. The moving truck was finally gone, and the neighborhood resumed its peaceful bliss. I go back to finish my routine and glimpse out the window when I return to bed. The top-floor window lights were on. She had only added those sheer white curtains, which were pulled back. I felt like a creeper; any minute, her husband would walk in and see her perverted neighbor leering at his wife. But I took the risk without rhyme or reason, except I wanted to get a better look at her.

I finally saw movement and switched off my light because that didn't make me look even creepier. She walked in and stopped right in front of the window. She wore a short black silk robe and pulled it up as she looked in the mirror. I don't know if she was judging her looks, but she was stunning from what I could see. She slowly untied her robe and let it fall off her shoulders. What was underneath was definitely meant for someone else. It was a black sheer lace bra and boy short set. I didn't realize I had stepped right into her view until I saw her look at me.

Oh shit!

I was frozen! I expected her to shriek like a banshee seeing her half-naked neighbor gawking into her bedroom or calling the cops. We locked eyes for what seemed like forever until she smirked before flicking her lights off. I'm still in shock about what happened. I look down and realize that I'm groping myself. I groaned, hoping I wasn't doing it while staring, but it felt so good.

"Great, just great." The most awkward part about this? Knowing I can't avoid meeting my new neighbor or neighbors...

Elivia

I WENT into town early to the little coffee shop I saw. Plus, I remember what Kelly said about a hot barista. Besides, who couldn't go for a steaming hot cup of Joe?

I threw on some leather leggings with a tan off-the-shoulder top and matching heels, found my plaid shawl, and hopped in my car that I had auto-started five minutes ago. It is essential when battling even the coldest of temperatures. My breath is visible as I try to lock my front door before freezing to death. I ease down my steps cautiously and glimpse at my peeping tom neighbor's house. The truck that was parked out front yesterday wasn't there. He must be an early riser, but what he wasn't was inconspicuous.

I'll admit that seeing him stare at me in my lace set was surprising, yet I felt a rush of adrenaline before I turned off my lights. Why wasn't I freaked out? Being in front of a camera has numbed me and made me enjoy the attention. It's a form of exhibitionism.

Besides, I have the last six years of my career in my dresser cabinet. It makes me feel like a bombshell. He proved my point when I saw his hand disappear below the windowsill. I smirk, thinking he rubbed one out, fantasizing about me.

This is crazy. I don't even know him! What I saw wasn't half bad, though. I know the official meeting will be awkward, given the circumstances. No matter: I'll deal with it when it happens.

Ding

"Good morning, and welcome to Coffee Heaven. What can I get you?"

Wow, Kelly wasn't kidding; he was hot. He was of average height, but his smile was perfect, and his green eyes were mesmerizing. I felt myself smiling like a high schooler, probably blushing like one.

I leaned forward to read his name tag, and he also seemed to inch forward. "Hello, Xavier." He holds out his hand, and I grab it, thinking he'd give it a friendly shake, but he kisses it ever so gently.

"Hello, beautiful. You must be new to our town. I would have noticed someone so radiant. What can I make for you?"

"Double shot espresso macchiato and a banana, please."

"Right away. You must be a city girl with such a fancy order. I usually don't make those, but I'll do my best to satisfy my new customer. So, how did Asher Falls get so lucky?" He faces the machine while preparing my drink.

"I'm working at the new Sugar Sweet boutique in the shopping center. I have dreamed of the small-town life since I lived in NYC, and now I have my perfect home in a quiet neighborhood. I know I'm going to love it here. How long have you been here?"

He slides over my order, "All my life, sweetheart. I don't think I could ever do big city living. Too much, too fast. Besides, I'm a big deal around here."

Is he flirting? Am I?!

"It was very fast paced." I chose to ignore the flirtation. He had potential, so we'll see.

"Well, I won't hold ya. Since I know where you work, I will surely see you around." I pay and leave a nice tip. "See you around," I say flirtatiously, or at least I hoped it was. I was never good at it.

When I got to my car, I set my cup in the holder, scanning for some decent music, thankful my seats were still warm and heating up as I searched. I hear a hiss and see a fire truck parking in the dirt lot. It's like a clown car but full of sexy, sweaty firemen. They're all in tactical gear as they enter the shop. Damnit! I knew I should have stayed there. I could have perused the catalog. But I must get to the boutique and introduce myself.

4

NICK

I'm surprised the Chief is treating us to coffee this morning. We came in at 5 a.m. to practice drill, which may have been our most sluggish response yet. We got into the practice house, extracted the family, and put out the fire in ten minutes when the average time was slightly over six. He screams, "Not good enough; what's the deal?"

Manning replies, "I need better than our cheap freeze-dried house coffee. I need a double, maybe a triple shot. I haven't recovered from the last call. Did they find out whose dumb ass kid had the party with the bonfire?"

"Yeah, Van Redding's kid. They sold his car and donated the money between our firehouse and the police department. Kid's going to the University of Chicago without his precious cherry red Camaro." We all laugh as we hop into the engine. We park in the dirt lot because the shop's parking lot is too small, and a car is already in a space. We don't want to damage that nice....Lexus. My mind knows because no one else has that specific type. Not many have a car of that caliber period, except the Van Redding's, who own the factory that makes all the delicious pastries in the tri-state area.

I match my steps with Bryson on the way to the door; he's a tree trunk of a firefighter. He's the big buff guy plastered on calendars with a tiny, adorable kitten that women buy ten copies of. I needed to confirm it was her without her seeing me. I'm not ready for the 'Nice to meet you, sorry I saw you half-naked while I touched myself' talk.

I peek around his torso and see her sipping her drink and messing with the dashboard. Suddenly, she looks in our direction, and I straighten back up to hide before rushing inside.

"You okay, Nicholas?" Bryson asks while ducking to clear the doorway. I tell you; he is massive. He doesn't need a ladder to rescue anything from a tree. "Huh, yeah, fine."

After we placed our orders, I slid over to the end of the counter where Xavier was working hard. "Hey, Xav, did a new girl come into the shop today?" I didn't want to seem too obvious.

"Oh, yeah. A stunningly gorgeous dirty blonde was here not long ago, but I didn't get her name. Ironic, huh?" As he jots all the names on the cups. "But I did find out she's working at that new lingerie shop at the center. I'm not surprised. She looks like she could model every sexy outfit, too. I don't even have a girl, but I'll be there for the opening."

Now, that's a bit of arousing information.

"Why, you interested?" He quickly interrupted my thoughts with that jarring question.

"She lives next door. I should know who's moving into my neighborhood."

"Perhaps checking out the competition? I heard you're finally entering the contest after all this time. They'd be happy to hear that." Referring to my parents.

I think I checked her out enough last night, but he did have a point; she could be another competitor in the contest.

"Yeah, right. Nobody's going to take that title from me."

"What about Mrs. Lindstat? She's been champion for the last three years."

"I'll respectfully wipe the floor with Mrs. Lindstat."

He chuckled, "Right. All right, fellas, orders are up!" Everyone grabs their cups and returns to the firehouse for more tedious training.

∾

Elivia

"Hello?" I walked into the quiet shop, but no one was in sight. I gauge the setup and see a few immediate changes that need to be made. The more 'advanced' lingerie was placed on the mannequins, but for such a small town, we should start slowly and perhaps put the bubble gum pink high-quality leather bondage set and electric red fur cuffs away for now. I'll need to call HQ and make suggestions from my immediate observation for future store openings.

"Hello?" I tried again.

"Oh, hello, sorry!" I hear a voice coming closer. "I was looking through the inventory to see if we can tame down some already set up displays." A cute, pixie-cut blonde girl with tortoiseshell glasses puts down a box to shake my hand. She looks like she's in awe. "Wow. You even dress like a gal from the big city. My name is Angellica. Pleased to meet you."

"Elivia, nice to meet you, too. I was thinking the same thing about the display. They won't come in if they see the Lover's deluxe leather bondage set. It's the holidays, so we should display the Mr. and Mrs. Claus set, the reindeer peek-a-boo jumper, the sexy Elf, and some common pieces. Did they send any holiday decorations?"

She pushes her frames up, "Not that I have seen, but I

haven't gone through all the boxes. There are so many! I hope we can open in time."

I set down my cup, purse, and shawl, walking around. The sound of my heels excites me sometimes. "It can be done. You've been here the past week and have done an incredible job. Now that I'm here, I can help finish the rest. If there are no decorations, it's no problem; I'll pick some up."

"Ohhh, probably not. I'm sure the store has been wiped clean by now. The annual holiday decorating competition is underway and is serious business in Asher Falls. You'd be lucky to find a candy cane around these parts."

Hmm, my competitive side is intrigued. I always loved the movies where friends who secretly love each other decorate the outside of one of their homes. Then the girl slips, he catches her, and they share their first kiss amidst the snow flurries.

"Elivia?" I snap out of my daydream to see Angellica looking concerned. "Oh, sorry, just thinking about one of those Hallmark movie scenarios. Anyway, I have plenty coming to my house and can always express ship more if necessary. This competition sounds like fun; maybe I should enter!"

"Well, go right ahead, but it can get vicious. I mean, it's no joke! Mrs. Lindstat won the last three years; before that was the Nicholas's, but..." Her face fell, and she clutched her chest dramatically. "Mr. Nicholas died, and not a week later, his wife died of a broken heart. It's...so sweet and tragic. Could you imagine a love so strong you follow each other into the after-life?" She wiped a tear away while swooning over their love story.

I felt my stomach drop and my heart flutter. "Sounds like they shared something extraordinary. I can only hope for a love like that."

"Me, too. I heard their son is entering the contest in their memory."

"Is there a formal sign-up?"

"Yeah, down at city hall. I think you better do it today; the deadline is tomorrow."

"Okay, only after we get this place set up. I'll work on the main display case, and you work on the showroom floor. Oh, make sure we have all available sizes on display. A woman of any size deserves to find something and feel beautiful. Let's get to it."

Ten hours later:

Whew! I am exhausted! We arranged the front display and made the floor all-inclusive in sizing options. We set up the dressing rooms, and I had enough time to run to city hall to enter the competition. The receptionist laughed and told me I was insane to try. I paid her no mind before walking away.

Once home, I noticed my neighbor's lights and his truck parked in the driveway. One of those country boy lifted trucks; you know?

I dropped my coat and purse at the door, went upstairs to strip, and stood under the high-pressure shower head for a minute. Everything is sore, especially my feet. It's the price we pay for stiletto heels.

I get out, freshly rejuvenated by Tony, my waterproof vibrator. He gets me through the dry spells. I slip on my festive satin emerald-green chemise and matching robe. Luckily, I left my heat running all day, so only the floors were chilly but felt soothing on my aching arches. I opened my living room curtains to see a few flurries floating around. I'm definitely hoping to wake up in a winter wonderland. I walk back to the fireplace and grab my phone to research how to start it. According to Google, I place three logs on the grate and light the kindling in the middle. Hmm, it seems simple enough.

As the kindling went, I walked into the kitchen to start heating up some chicken and wild rice soup. I also started some water for hot cocoa. After pouring the dry contents into the pot and hot water to cover, I mix it to look more like soup and less like a tan lump in water. I'm bouncing around to my music as I'm stirring. I couldn't wait to cozy up and...

BEEP! BEEP! BEEP!

My smoke alarm goes off, but I'm not burning the soup.

THE FIREPLACE!!!!!

I whip around to see smoke billowing into my living room and creeping into the kitchen. I don't even know if I have a fire extinguisher! Panicked, I opened the door by the kitchen and frantically looked around as the alarm blared.

"OMG! OMG! OMG! ***Cough cough*** Where is the extinguisher?! ***cough*** AHHHH! I'm going to burn my house down!"

The alarm is screeching, and so am I.

I'm sure the police and fire department will be here any minute to see the ditz who burned her house down.

Then, before I could comprehend it, someone was in my house! I heard a whooshing sound and saw the smoke turn thick and white. I leaned against the island, running my fingers through my hair, my heart pounding. I hear them coughing.

"Are you okay?!" I screamed. I didn't need a dead person added to my already embarrassing story.

"I'm ***cough*** fine; stay there or go outside. I'm opening the windows to ***cough cough*** let the smoke out." I heard a squeaking noise and saw the panes being raised, and the smoke started to clear up faster.

"You probably forgot to open the flue before starting the fire."

The deep voice comes from the living room, making this official meeting even more awkward because he's only in his boxers and rubber boots, not even a coat, even though it's barely double digits outside. He was sweaty and panting... and I was staring at his bulge. The adrenaline must have made him...ahem...or maybe because I'm half naked and breathing hard, I quickly wrap the robe tightly around me. He sets the extinguisher down while staring at me. Perhaps that didn't help.

"Umm, thanks so much. I should probably wait for the fire department."

"I intercepted dispatch and told them to cancel the call. There's no need to break their sleep when I'm equipped to handle it. No flames, no real damage."

"I guess I should hire a professional to work on my fireplace. Obviously, I don't know what I'm doing. Where are my manners? My name is Elivia."

"Nick. If you want, I can light it for you; if I'm not at the firehouse, I usually do a 5/2 week and sometimes a 4/3. I don't mind."

"I'm sorry, I don't know what that means." I'm pretty sure I had that deer-in-the-headlights look.

He laughed; his smile was gorgeous. "Sorry, it means I'm on call for five days with two days off. Technically, I'm on call now, but the firehouse is being fumigated, so I'm home this rotation and responding to emergencies from here. Like this one. As soon as I heard the address, I rushed right over."

I cringed but then smelled my soup, turning around to ensure it wasn't burning; that would be the icing on this already shameful situation. "Would you like some soup or hot chocolate to warm up?"

Since you're technically naked, hard, and drenched in my kitchen, a sexy fireman lives next door to me. What...luck.

"As tempting as that sounds, I'm not exactly dressed for it, plus I'm still on call and can't be...distracted." His eyes raked over me once more.

You look perfectly undressed to me.

Stop it, Elivia! Seriously!

I shake out of my daydream, and he smiles, "You can close your windows in five to ten minutes. Nice to meet you, Elivia."

"You too, Nick." He grabs the extinguisher and walks out. I

watch him trek over to his open door and shut it. He walked normally, like it wasn't freezing outside. Now I've seen him half naked from far away and up close. I'm going to need another session with Tony. I think he might be bigger than Tony. I consider Tony to be average size of like five inches, but he was well equipped to get the job done with his multiple vibrating speeds and patterns. With the right combination, he sends me into bliss. But now I'm fantasizing about his...

Okay, why am I thinking about that?!

Two minutes later, I see the smoke is almost gone, so I close all the windows. Tomorrow is another day, and hopefully, my shipment will come in. I rush-shipped additional decorations and split them between my house and the shop.

I'm startled out of my thoughts by a knock on the door. It's Nick and he still has no clothes on. Is he teasing me on purpose?

"Just in case." He hands me a small extinguisher.

This time, I don't cover up and shift my body against the door, giving him a peek at my thigh. He eyes me up and down once more. "Have a good night, Elivia."

God, the way he says my name in that guttural tone. "Thanks again for saving me." I put it under the sink, eat, clean up, and put stuff away before I head upstairs. I yawn and stretch before slipping off the robe and pulling my comforter back. Before I get in, I look up, yet again, I'm met with his gaze. This time, I wave before I turn off my light and get comfortable as he stands there for a bit longer before his lights go off.

The following day, I tell Angellica I'll be in around noon. I was finally notified that my delivery was coming between 7 and 9 a.m. I ordered like $500 worth of decorations, but I love Christmas! I started with what I had, which was the holiday welcome mat and snow-flocked wreath. I'm happy with my little progress as I step back and send a selfie to my parents. I lower my phone, and my mouth drops as I take a real good look at my other neighbor's decorations. The whole neighborhood was out and setting up their homes, and we're not talking about a string of white lights and a candy cane arch. One house has an animatronic Santa and his reindeer on the roof. It slides forward as if launching to the next house as he greets you with a hearty 'Ho Ho Ho!' They also have huge light ornament archways. Next to them, the neighbor has a different theme. They chose white and gold, from their lights to the mini tree forest and tree toppers. They even projected it onto their house so, at night, it'll look like a snow flocked spectacular. I am in awe, "Wow, I have got to get serious if I want to win this."

"Win what?"

"AHHHH!" I jump, turn around, and see Nick behind me. "Why would you do that?!" I shriek angrily, having almost dropped the coffee that I had made.

"I forgot to tell you last night that when I opened the flue, it looked like it needed a good cleaning. The Landon's rarely used it and have been out of that house at least a year."

I exhale forcefully to diffuse my anger. "Oh. Thanks, I'll look for a chimney sweep before work."

"So, you were talking about winning something?"

I thought it was weird he was so concerned about what I was mumbling. "Yeah, I heard about the town's contest and decided to enter. Now, I see how serious the neighborhood is taking it."

"That's because the reigning champion lives over there." He points to the Santa house. I should have known. They spent big bucks on that piece alone.

It's not always about how much you spend but the emotions you feel!

"Well, there's a new opponent in town, and I aim to win!"

He scoffed and pointed, "With what? That cheap straw doormat and shoddy wreath?! That's hilarious!"

He was laughing too hard for my liking. "No. This is what I

have unpacked. I have more coming! I don't see you winning with your army of tacky, plastic snowmen. How original!" I couldn't help but return the favor by laughing obnoxiously in his face, but he didn't reciprocate; in fact, he walked away.

"What did I say? Nick!"

5

NICK

She didn't know my backstory or how every snowman represented every member of my family. Positioning them as if they were in the formal room singing carols and using a recording to play in the background. My mom loved it when we all gathered at the family home and would break out singing during the tree trimming and end the night trying to recite the 12 days of Christmas. Mom is the one who always gave us clues before the next refrain.

Those precious memories made me want to try harder. To make them proud, it was the rebirth of our family tradition. I wasn't letting the new girl stroll in with her fancy car and take the trophy.

I slammed the door and growled my frustration out loud while checking my phone to make sure there were no missed emergency calls. Seeing none, I paced the living room. I needed to blow off some steam and what better way than to bring the stuff down from the attic? I have two boxes full of lights, garland, and decor for the tree. I'll recreate all our cherished family memories outside and use my parent's tale as the central theme. Everyone knows their tragically beautiful love story. I'll win with raw emotion. They barely know Elivia exists. I shouldn't worry about some irrelevant nobody. I peek outside to see a delivery truck in her driveway, and they are bringing boxes in as she signs the release.

I scoff, "Game on, Elivia." Just because she was beautiful... sexy...downright alluring. *ahem*

She wasn't going to distract me, but I did notice a frown and sadness in her demeanor, which reminded me of how coldly I reacted. Did I go too far?

~

Elivia

I NEED help getting through the boutique door with these boxes. "Angellica! A little help!"

She jogs from around the counter, "Oh my, how much did you spend?!"

Once the boxes were down, I grabbed the garland and wrapped it around her whimsically. "What're a few dollars for holiday cheer?! I want people drawn to our window like the Macy's display in New York City."

"Ooh! I've always wanted to see that! It looks so magical." She swoons as she pulls out the artificial snow blanket to place it on the window ledge.

"It is the most magical display you'll ever see. We'll take a road trip one day. Right now, I love the peace here. It's my small-town love story coming to life. Now, all I need is someone to fall in love with."

"Any potentials? You've only been here a few days, but word gets out. Xavier asked me about you this morning. He seems interested!" She squealed in excitement.

"He's definitely hot, but I didn't feel that spark, unlike with..." I trailed off because I was still unsure about what happened earlier. I think I offended him, but I only fired back after he ragged on my decor. Maybe it was too much New York. I became the stereotypical rude New Yorker, and I felt terrible. I don't know how to make amends.

"Uhh, never mind, we're behind. Turn on the music, and let's get to work; the flyers will arrive with the mailer tomorrow, so everyone knows about the grand opening on Saturday."

"Do you think people will recognize you?"

"Recognize me? What do you mean?" I tried to sound nonchalant, but I'm pretty sure she could tell I was shaken.

"I mean, will they know you were one of the top lingerie models for the company opening this store? Come on, I looked you up to find out who I was working with and saw you basically headlined their catalog. You're a supermodel! The only change is the cut and color of your hair." She stated so casually. I thought it was quite a difference, but I might be wrong. I guess we'll find out at the grand opening.

"I'm not a supermodel, just a catalog one. And I moved to get away from being immediately recognized. So, I hope not. The chances are minuscule."

"It may be a quiet town, but we're not prudes. The Jones have seven kids. And we are opening up this type of store here."

I sat there a bit frazzled; she may be right. I don't want to be recognized or asked out because of what I used to do; it's not genuine.

We look around a few hours later and bask in our hard work. It looks like the North Pole was built here, and the elves were here to help customers find the perfect piece of lingerie. They were greeted by the Mrs. Claus set complete with fur hoodie and shawl, a close replica to the one I wore in the issue, except mine was way shorter with a cherry red thong. This length was for the more domesticated woman and had red velvet boy shorts. It still gave off that racy vibe.

"Alright, take tomorrow off; you've gone above and beyond. Plus, Saturday is going to be quite an interesting day."

"Great, I can start my own decorating for the contest. I only have an apartment, but there's a category for that, too." I give her the excess decorations to increase her chances.

OH! I'm so glad to be home. I slip into my long silk dress with the daring split and set the robe down nearby. It seems normal to slip on something so risqué and sexy, but it might look like I'm trying too hard to the average person. I've spent much of my adult life prancing around in them. For me, it's second nature.

Knock knock

"Morty's Tree delivery."

I put on my robe and answer the door. When I do, I'm met with a freezing cold blast and see a few flurries. The following week or so has a high chance of substantial snow. I shuddered as the two men brought in my six-and-a-half-foot Douglas; it was full and fragrant. While they placed it in the tree stand, I light my cinnamon-scented candles for a beautiful festive combination.

After they set it up and left, I put on some holiday tunes. I drag a few boxes over and look through them. My theme would be a taste of NYC. I would decorate the front in this year's Macy's display signature colors. My friend Dylan told me this year's theme colors were cherry red, vintage gold, and forest green. I started with the lights, then the ribbons and bows to fill the tree. After that, I filled it in with beautiful hand-carved ornaments. It was a masterpiece!

I shut off the house lights and plugged them in to gauge my progress. The illumination made me tear up a little. I shiver but don't want to take the chance of burning my house down again. I would cuddle up under my heavy winter blanket after I was done.

Knock knock

"Who could that be?" Maybe the delivery guys forgot something, but I'm pleasantly surprised to see Nick outside and open my door immediately, slightly disappointed to see he's fully dressed.

"Nick...umm, what are you doing here?"

He looks down before he reaches into his coat and pulls out a bottle of wine. "I wanted to welcome you officially and offer to start your fireplace. It's going to feel close to zero by morning."

"Oh, thank you. Perfect timing: I was freezing! Come in; I would love that. Maybe I'll sleep down here instead." I saw him eyeing my clothing choice, then turning to the fireplace. I take the bottle into the kitchen to open it. I pour us both a glass, mine a little less because red wine steals all my inhibitions. For ordinary people, it's tequila or vodka. Not me; I can drink those like water, but a glass or two of red wine, and I'm ready to hump the closest hottie, and luckily for me or not, he was in my living room.

I returned, and he started the fire, concentrating hard on the task. "Here you go." I hand him the glass, and he sets it down while he ensures he's got a good roar going. The heat radiating from the fire felt terrific.

"Thanks. Have you been fiddling with this?" He raised his brow.

"Are you kidding? Since almost burning down my place the first time? No way, I'll leave that to the professionals." I settled down, and the sash loosened and showed more of the top of the gown. I saw his subtle reaction, causing me to cross my legs and watch his eyes wander down. He quickly tends the fire and takes a heavy sip. Awkward silence took over until he set the poker down and sat on the couch across from me with his glass.

"So, tell me, Elivia, what brings you to Asher Falls?"

I tip my glass, "Living my dream. Finally, I got the small town setting I've been looking for. Spent my life in Chicago and New York City. I'm over it."

"So, it's just you living here?"

"Yes, it's just me...is that okay with you?" I raise my brow.

He stumbles, "Yeah...yeah, I assumed you were attached even though I never saw anyone else. I thought maybe he was away on business. Leaving his wife to tend to the home." He sipped while observing me. I should feel offended by that last statement. What is this, Little House on the Prairie?

"Huh, any other part of my life you put together in your little fantasy?" I lean forward and rest my arm on my crossed leg. That question caught him off guard.

"I, uh, I wasn't fantasizing..." His eyes darted left and right.

I decided to test that theory as I opened my robe, revealing that the split exposed my upper thigh with my legs crossed. I could already tell that even one glass was too much for me because his gaze lit fire to my core. I watched him for only a moment before he looked away.

"I was trying to figure out your story. This didn't seem like your speed, and then you go and enter the town's famed holiday competition, not knowing how ruthless and cutthroat it can be."

"I think I have a good chance of winning..."

Nick

"I THINK I have a good chance of winning..." She states arrogantly. She has no idea.

"Strong words from fresh meat." Shit, I shouldn't have used that term. I sound like a predator.

She quirked her brow and folded her arms, "You don't think I can win?"

"Ha! I don't even think you'll place. The tree is nice, but these people, including myself, have worked on their designs year-round, and there's no way we're letting some new tart come in and steal it." I didn't realize I was standing until she stood in response.

"I'm going to wipe the floor with you! Maybe I'll put the trophy in a high-visibility area, like my bedroom window. You know where that is, don't you?"

That took the wind out of my sails. I stood there in silence while Elivia chuckled, finishing her glass.

"I have to go." With no comeback, I put on my jacket as fast as possible to leave, but before I could reach the door, I felt her hand on my arm stop me and turn me around.

She's so close and smells like heaven; I could smell her past the pine and cinnamon wafting throughout her home. It's the soft and delicate scent of Jasmine.

"Wait, Nick, that was unnecessary. I'm sorry about the incident outside when I made fun of your display and now. I didn't mean to offend you."

Her face softened, and I could tell she was sincere. "It's... fine...I didn't mean to get so defensive. There's a long story behind my purpose, but maybe another time. Enjoy that fire, and keep the extinguisher nearby, just in case. Goodnight, Elivia."

I didn't even give her a chance to respond. I raced across the yards to the sanctity of my house. I closed the door and leaned against it, running my fingers through my hair with one hand and palming myself with the other.

Fuck! What is she doing to me?!

She riles me up with that smart-ass mouth and pushes my buttons, especially when she brings up my peeping. All I could think about was pinning her against the wall next to the fireplace and taking her. She didn't know how badly I wanted to explore every inch of her. I needed to leave before I reacted. I couldn't grasp how serious her teasing was; maybe she was naturally flirtatious.

She was a very sexy distraction, but I needed to focus, and *when* I win and place it on my mantle, I'll make her look at it while I thrust against her and claim her as my prize. I growl as I live in my fantasy. I concede to my room and see the glow from her living room. Maybe she did decide to sleep downstairs.

I'm so stiff; my imagination is running wild, and I can only think about her. Since I can't have her yet, I have to take care of my own needs. I go to my bedroom and grab my Sugar Sweet catalog. I'm going to close my eyes and have her in my fantasies.

6

ELIVIA

The mailer looked fantastic in this morning's paper! It was sexy yet subtle. I compared my old look with my current one and didn't think I was that recognizable. I guess we'll see.

I spent lunch with Kelly, finally getting to thank her for her hard work in realizing my dream home. We eat at this little Mexican restaurant, Tres Amigos, and even though it's 30 degrees outside, we treat ourselves to extra-large frozen margaritas.

"Elivia, I'm so glad you've settled in. What do you think of Asher Falls?"

"It's a dream come true! Beautiful views, peace, quiet, and friendly people. Plus, this town has healthy competition regarding this decorating contest."

"Yeah, it's brutal and in no way healthy." We chuckle.

"I see. I'm curious about one contestant. Actually, he's my neighbor."

"Is he cute?!" I feel like she's toying with me. She should know everyone in town. And how was I supposed to answer that when trying to be discreet? "He's handsome, but he seems very serious about this contest. He said there was a story behind his reason to enter."

"Who is it?"

"Umm, his name is Nick. He's a firefighter..."

"Oh, I know Nick. I knew that was his neighborhood, but I hadn't been to his house. He and my husband are close friends; he always goes there. Nick is a good guy but has a tragic past. His dad died some years ago, and not a week later after his death did his mom die of a broken heart. It's sad and beautiful at the same time. Anyway, they were decorating champions six years in a row. When they passed, Nick avoided everything Christmas; he didn't even decorate his house. His dark home against the lit neighborhood was such a somber statement. I'm glad he's somewhat back to normal and functioning. This is the first year he's returned to the competition. I assume whatever he displays will be a tribute to his parents."

That is the same story Angellica told me, so this was common knowledge. I couldn't even imagine. How would I even function? I made fun of his display, and now I feel like crap.

"Whatever you're feeling, make sure you're certain. The last two girls were literal nightmares. You know..." She smiled wide, and I felt like she was up to something. "He's at the shopping center, volunteering as the mall Santa! The whole firehouse is there. Let's go see if you're on Santa's naughty list!"

"What?! No, that's ridiculous."

"My hubby is an elf, and I need photographic proof for blackmailing purposes. I've been begging for this Tiffany necklace, and this will definitely help. Come on! Maybe when you're on Santa's lap, you'll feel his...sack!" She laughs disturbingly loud, causing people to look at us.

Shoot me now.

"Okay, okay, shh!"

"Let's get you a *very* Merry Christmas!"

We arrive at the shopping center, walking past the boutique, and I'm elated to see people looking at our display in curiosity.

In the center of the square was Santa's North Pole setup, complete with a 20 or 30-foot tree decked to the nines; it was breathtaking. At the base were some oversized presents, ornaments, and a big sleigh with Santa sitting in the middle. The line was almost non-existent, perhaps because it was the middle of a weekday. Kelly waves wildly in their general direction, getting the attention of some of the guys. I was curious, "Which one is your husband?"

"Over there, standing next to Nick, no doubt complaining about this. Nick whispered to him, and now he won't look this way. Oh my God, they have him in striped tights! Green striped tights! HA! This is priceless!" She takes a succession of photos.

I second-guessed my outfit of a black tunic, patterned tights, and knee-high boots. I totally regret my red pea coat; it stands out like a drop of blood in the snow. Nick's eyes raked over me like a moth to a flame as we got closer.

"Ho! Ho! Ho! Merrrrrrrrry Christmas!" He bellows, fully immersing himself in the role.

A cute little girl hopped off with a big smile, waving happily as she reached for her mom's hand with a candy cane in the other.

We were next! Kelly walks up, points my way, and then she leans in and whispers in his ear. He nods and hands her a candy cane before she gets up, trying to take a selfie with her husband. He was not having it. She gave up and returned to where I was stuck in that spot.

"Go on, your turn!" She nudges me forward. I couldn't even figure out what she may have said. That gives him the upper hand on me.

Oh, how I wish those hands were on me.

I approach slowly.

"Ho! Ho! Ho! Come on up, little girl. Santa doesn't bite..."

What if I want you to?

I can't believe I thought that. I slowly slid onto Santa's lap. "OOF!" He huffs, and I almost jump off his lap, but he holds me down firmly. "Relax, Santa's teasing. Have you been a good girl for Christmas?"

I notice his hand moving up my thigh, and I gasp when he bounces his knee; it sends a jolt down my spine between my legs. "Y-yes, I have."

"Good, now tell Santa what you want?" His voice dropped a few octaves, almost like he was growling.

Is that how he asked anyone else? Or was he teasing me?

"Well, Santa, what I want doesn't come in a box. It's a connection, a feeling that ultimately gives me the perfect fairy-tale moment. But first, it starts with a kiss."

He's staring at my lips and suddenly clears his throat. I feel something under my leg that was not there moments before; I look down and grin.

"Santa will see what he can do about that. You know, you barely made my good-girl list. I know about the fireplace incident..." He tsks, and I giggle.

"Ohhh...I'm so sorry, Santa. I'll try to be daddy's, Santa's good girl. Bye!" I grab the candy cane in his hand, hop off, and wave. I turn back to see him shift in his suit.

Jackpot!

I saunter away but can't help but laugh.

Nick

HER REMARK SPARKED MY CURIOSITY. Could she be interested in...no, I can't think about that now. I'm throbbing, and it's painful. I need a break to cool down, and I definitely need rum for this eggnog.

"So, that's the new girl?' Beckham sits down, and his shoe bells jingle. I laughed before shrugging, "Yeah, my neighbor and my competition. The contest comes first. I will not be distracted. It took me forever to get the set up perfect."

"Great timing, too; the general public will be coming by for people's choice tonight."

I got up extra early this morning to guarantee my entry into the competition was ready. Once I got just the right sentimental holiday music playing, I looked over everything else. The lights and icicles offset the main yard display, and at the end, an "In loving memory" with our last holiday photo would tug at the heartstrings.

She was still hanging her stuff up when I left for this work obligation, so she may not be ready for the foot traffic, which works to my advantage.

No votes for you, new girl.

I'm going straight home after her teasing me at the shopping center. That sly smile was lethal and held so much promise.

After the competition, Nick. Then you can make her yours in every way.

I recall her wish. I didn't expect something so profound. She sounds like she was looking for one of those Christmas happily ever afters.

It's less than an hour before onlookers start appearing in our neighborhood. With a past and current champion, this place will be packed. I turn down our street and come to a screeching halt.

Her house was...immaculate! It showcased her NYC roots with plenty of reds, greens, and gold that matched her tree, which was gorgeous. I didn't want to let on when I was there. The outside archways had big, beautiful bows and lights paving the way to her candy cane-striped door. The cheap wreath and mat were gone and replaced with giant gift boxes, and they all came together with simple white lights.

"Son of a bitch!" I hit the gas and sped into my driveway. I needed to turn on my lights and start the music before I got cleaned up.

I couldn't believe I might actually lose to her!

No way was I going to let that happen. I had to do something. But what? I paced my entryway, looking for something, anything!

I...I...I could trip the breaker.

Just a friendly prank.

Yeah, no permanent damage!

My internal conversation convinced me that it wasn't a big deal. I camouflaged myself in a black Henley and jeans. I snuck over to the rear of her home, where I assumed the outside lights were plugged in. I was right; she connected them to a surge protector, which keeps the main circuit breaker from... tripping. I unplug the surge protector and plug the lights directly into the house. The lights immediately flickered, then went dark.

Success! I knew the power capacity of her smaller home was lesser than that of a house like mine. Victorious, I plug in my display with Dean Martin leading the Christmas classics. Her house resembled mine when I was in mourning. People will think she doesn't care. I change and pop in some cookies for extra incentive. They'd be ready about ten minutes before the official start time.

I look outside to see the headlights signal she just got home. Hometown hero, one...new girl, zero.

7

ELIVIA

WHAT IN THE JINGLE BELL HELL?!
I come home, and it's a dark void among the festival of lights. I get in quickly and check my breaker and see it tripped. How can that be? I used surge protectors. I slip on my winter boots to trudge out back. My stepdad taught me many things, from auto mechanics to house maintenance. He said he always wanted me to feel safe in fixing things that seemed overwhelming. He was so patient with me, and I am thankful. He always said to troubleshoot outside and work your way inside. I walk out my door with a flashlight pointing toward the back of my house.

I see the surge protector tossed on the ground and not plugged in. In fact, the plug is connected directly to my house, which caused my breaker to pop, but who...

I flash my light toward the ground by the outlet and see footprints. Much larger prints than mine going toward... Nick's house!

ARE YOU KIDDING ME?!?!

"That prick sabotaged my display!" I am fuming; how could

he stoop so low? I thought he was a nice guy, even someone I wouldn't mind having dinner with!

Un-freaking-believable!

I plug everything in safely and go inside to reset the breaker. I was going to turn it back on immediately but decided against it. I put my other boots on from earlier and stomp over to his place. I work up some tears before frantically knocking.

Knock knock knock knock knock

I knock frantically to seem desperate. I hear Nick's footsteps. It takes the strength of the abominable snowman not to punch him in the balls and prance away.

"Uh, Elivia, hey. What's wrong?" He avoids looking at my house.

"I-I don't know what happened, but my lights won't work! Were they on when you got home?"

He glances over quickly, then scratches his head, "Umm, I don't think they were. Did you check the fuses or the breaker?"

Of course, you lying bastard, my daddy taught me well, but you don't know that.

"I think so, but nothing! What am I supposed to do? The judging starts soon!" I sounded panicked and doubled up on the tears, putting my hand on my hip and sighing hard. I ran my hand through my hair.

"Do you...Do you think someone would sabotage me? They said it was cutthroat, but what low-life, evil, pathetic person would stoop so low?"

I laid it on pretty thick. His ears were as red as Rudolph's nose after a cold. He wanted to answer, but he knew.

"I, uh...I don't know."

"Oh? Because judging by the ginormous boot prints leading from my house to yours, I'd say you got a pretty big fucking clue as to who did!"

His hands shot up, "Elivia, it was a prank, I swear. I didn't mean any harm."

"Didn't mean any harm?! You want people to vote for you with the sweet, emotional story of your parent's love, but they would be so disappointed in your actions!" I saw him flinch; I may have gone too far, but he forced this!

I sigh and pinch my nose, "That was too far, but so was what you did! You want a war, Nicholas, you got it!"

I turn around and walk back to my house.

Game on.

~

Nick

I DIDN'T EXPECT her to explode like that. I know New Yorkers are abrasive or brash. Maybe I overreacted to her display and sabotaged her out of fear, fear I could lose.

I had to clear my mind for the walk-throughs. I decided to wear my Santa suit and plated the cookies when I heard the timer. When I step outside, her display is up and running. It is simply beautiful.

I see a lot of townspeople on our street walking around. I can hear the oohs and ahhs as they start on the opposite side of the road, working their way around.

The Kensington's are the first to stop by with their two kids. "Mark, Pam, good to see you. Wow, is that Maxim and Emery? You guys have grown so much!"

"Nick, glad to see this beautiful tribute to your parents."

"Thank you, Pam. Walk around and immerse yourself in a moment in time. Have some cookies, kids. Santa insists!" They were the first of many in awe and happy to see me competing again. I have popularity and familiarity on my side.

Then my guys stopped by in the fire engine. Sirens and all.

Subtle.

"Wow, sexy Santa, kickass display!" Beck hops off the back and slaps my back.

"Thanks, Beck. I feel good. I think...Mom and Dad would approve."

"Yeah, they would. So, where is that hot neighbor of yours?"

"Uhh, over there." I point but realize the others are staring in that direction with wide-open mouths.

Then Beck turns his head, and his jaw drops, "Hot damn! Kelly would kill me if she saw me looking at something like that."

I look over, and Elivia is in a provocative Mrs. Claus outfit. It was a fitted red velvet hoodie dress with white fur trim, accessorized with red gloves and black velvet thigh-high boots. When she bent over, it left very little to the imagination. It was super scandalous and fucking sexy as hell. Now, I matched their gawking.

Oh, Mrs. Claus... you are working toward my naughty list. You deserve to be thrown over my lap and spanked red.

"Holy fuck, Nicholas, who is that?" I hear Perry ask as he whispers to Jackson, who attempted to take a photo from far away. After several disappointing tries, he shoves it in his pocket, "Screw it, I'm going over there. It's going to be much better up close and personal anyway." I heard a few agree as they skipped my display and headed over her way. I can hear her giggling and laughing with the people viewing her display, including my entire company.

Playing up the sex kitten routine. Well played. I even found myself following my group. Walking a few yards to her walkway. She giggles and waves to us. "Ooh, firefighters! I love a strong man who can rescue a damsel in distress. Merry Christmas, boys. Welcome to a little piece of New York City! Mrs. Claus welcomes you with a sweet treat and a sneak peek. Oops!" She says as she bends over, presenting her plate of confectionery delights.

I should be standing behind her. I'd leave a handprint on her delicious round ass so prominent to mark my territory to the masses as she moans my name.

"My name is Elivia, and if you like my...display, which I know you do, don't forget to vote for me! Take a walk-through; I'm sure you'll be pleased." Then she giggles like a schoolgirl. Why does that turn me on so fucking much? I didn't even know I was following them until she stepped in front of me.

"Coming to destroy my display this time?"

"Elivia..."

"Save it, Santa! I don't want you on my property, period. I can't believe I thought you were a good guy; you even saved my life! I thought... I thought you were a nice guy." She sounded disappointed not only with me but with herself because she let her guard down.

"I..." She turned around and walked away without giving me a chance. The view was better than I could even imagine, but I couldn't enjoy it. I didn't know what to say, so I slunk back to my yard and tried to push the guilt down while entertaining the crowd. It went well, and the contest ended at 10 p.m. and would every night for several days.

I couldn't get myself back into the spirit with the guilt. She looked so festive and happy in the presence of people, but during the lulls, her smile disappeared, and every time we exchanged looks, she shook her head. Smooth move, Santa!

8

ELIVIA

Oh, this is too much fun! Was I mad at Nick for pulling the prank? Only for a moment, but I knew I could use it to my advantage and make him feel guilty. It was clever, I'll give him that.

The Mrs. Claus outfit? I saw him walking out of his room in his costume. I scrambled to find his counterpart and put it on. Call it temptation, just out of his reach. But that wouldn't be the end of the prank war. Nothing was going to distract me from paying him back.

The following day, I was heading to my car when I saw Nick outside replacing bulbs. "Good morning, Nick! Have a great day!" I laid it on thick and waved before I got in my car. He looked so confused, but a smile also appeared. I'm sure he felt terrible, but when I spoke, it made him feel like he was in the clear.

HA!

Be afraid, Nick, be very afraid.

I changed my focus because the mailer was out, and the store was opening to the public today! I wore red pants and a green blouse to celebrate the holiday spirit. I even wore my mom's silly holiday bell earrings. Occasionally, I put them on, take a picture, and send it to her. It warms her heart, and that's all that matters. I zoom out so she can see the store in the background and smile wide, sending it with the caption, "Merry Christmas, I love you."

When I open the door, it smells like freshly baked gingerbread men, and the spirit of the holidays is in the air. I love it!

"Angellica! Hey!"

"Hi! Don't you love the gingerbread scent?"

"I do, but I love your festive dress with gingerbread men on it even more! Are you ready?" She twirled in her fabulous holiday threads. She was like the little sister I always wanted.

"Absolutely! Let me start the music, and you can look around before we open the doors."

∾

THIRTY MINUTES LATER:

"Merry Christmas, everyone! Our names are Elivia and Angellica; we will be Santa's helpers today. Welcome to Sugar Sweet Lingerie. 'Tis the season to buy yourself something sweet. We have a size for every beautiful face here! So, shop around and find the perfect gift for your Santa to unwrap. Thank you!"

The best feeling is seeing a woman confidently walking around with a beautiful piece of lingerie. The confidence to know that she will put it on and feel sexy, not only for someone but for herself. Would I love a man to wear these for? Yes. To have big, strong arms wrapped around my waist as I'm thrown on the bed and for that lingerie to end up on the floor? Absolutely, a girl can dream, can't she?

I walk around, observing some smiling faces and some who might be blushing.

"Well, hello again, beautiful." I turn to see Xavier with a

rose in his hand. He was handsomely dressed in all black. "Congratulations to you on the grand opening."

"Oh, thank you, it's beautiful! What are you doing here? Shopping for a pretty little lady?" I walk around a display, and he follows.

"No...unless I was buying something for you."

Wow. Bold, isn't he?

"Yeah, well, I already own this entire line. I do work for them, you know."

"Well, that's nice to know. Perhaps one day, I'll be able to hold the merchandise."

I could only raise my brow. "Well, sir. One step at a time."

He jerks and grabs his phone, "Oh, sorry, got to take this. We will set something up, alright?" He taps my chin, causing me to smile. I'll deal with that down the road.

I spot Kelly walking around with the evergreen set. It's a sheer corset and G-string, perfect for her slightly curvier figure.

"Hey, Livi, let me ask you; I'm looking for something kinkier than what's on display. Would you happen to have a restraining set? I have a bit of curiosity."

"Color me impressed. Well, you are in luck. We do have a beginner bondage set that will work for you. Let me go in the back and grab it. What do you want, black or red?"

"Ooh, give me fire engine red, please."

I retrieved the set and a bonus gift with her purchase.

"Surprise!" I brought out the set and placed the surprise on top.

"Is that a tassel whip?"

"Oh yeah, I suspect you'll like the feeling, especially while surrendering your control. I want the deets about it later."

"You know it. Thanks, girlie!" She heads to the checkout line.

Then the door rings, and I hear male voices, a lot of them. I look over to see the firefighters strolling around.

Now, isn't this interesting?

Nick

I DON'T WANT to go to the grand opening of the lingerie store, but they are forcing me. Kelly told Beck, who told the ENTIRE group, that our little city gal has a crush on me. And I don't know if it's true or if Kelly is hopeful after witnessing the last two train wrecks, but it's the talk of the firehouse. Why? Because they have nothing else to do while waiting for the next call.

The shop is nice. It looks like a winter wonderland and smells fantastic. Every item I see displayed; I visualize her in it. For all I know, she owned every piece from the catalog. She seemed very comfortable slipping on something sexy for herself because I hadn't seen her in anything but, especially in my fantasies.

"Hello, Nick." I'm shaken out of my thoughts by her soft voice. She looked very festive, like a beautifully wrapped gift in a Christmas bow. Ready for Santa to...deliver.

"Hey, Elivia. You... look nice. Congrats on the store's opening."

She looks around, "Thanks for coming out and for the support. Well, thanks to your entire team or company? What do you call a group of firefighters anyway?"

"A pretty hot calendar."

Oh my God, why did I say that?!

But instead of a nasty look, she's laughing. "That was funny...can't wait to get one. So, are you at the station today doing your 5/2, or what was it? 4/3 shift thing?"

"Umm, no, just a regular training day. I'll be home later. You need me to light your fireplace?"

Among other things...

"I might. I'll let you know."

"Okay."

"AFFD, time to go!" My Chief bellows from the outside, not like anyone was buying anything. If they valued their lives, all the married guys already got gifts for their wives. And us singles, well, it'd look pretty odd buying anything in here. I was in support, and they were here to see some sort of show. Sorry, fellas, that will be done behind closed doors.

"Well, got to run. Maybe I'll see you later."

"Yeah, thanks."

I noticed she had a rose in her hand; that could be a sign of competition, or maybe I'm reading too much into it. I look back and give her a smile. I hope we resolved the prank fiasco.

～

Elivia

OH NO, this is not over until I exact my revenge. I cannot wait to see the look on his face.

I arrived home about an hour earlier than usual to make sure my display was intact. I put nothing past him now.

I had the cover of winter's early sunsets to sneak around, adding a few items to his display and a sign. It only took 15 minutes to set up.

I didn't bother to cover my tracks. Why? He didn't! I baked a fresh batch of cookies and slipped into my elf costume. I put on the green bodysuit, sliding the zipper slightly over my cleavage, you know, to keep it PG. I added a gold pennant belt and matching wrist decor. Finishing up with the hat and, of course, shoes with bells. Elivia, the enchanting Elf, was ready to snag some votes. And also, to see the look on his face! I had my phone ready to record the moment of my sweet victory!

9

NICK

"One alarm fire at the logging mill! Frank says it's in the storage lot!" The Chief yelled over the PA as he slammed down the phone. I ran to my suit, pulled it up, grabbed my coat, and ran down to grab the rest of my gear before hopping on the engine, pulling away, sirens blaring. We were out and on our way in less than 90 seconds.

When we are near the mill, the Chief starts barking orders, "Perry, Jackson, I want you at the rear with the attack hoses! If you can get inside, find the source and radio back! Beckham, take the lead in front; the night shift workers have been accounted for. Nicolas, man the ladder hose!"

I ran into the ladder cabin to position it at the fire and wait for the signal. I saw Beckham use his ax to cut down the door. It usually takes him five swings or less, this time a record-breaking three. Davis ran into the unknown with his hose on full blast. The thick white smoke was immediate as he disappeared into it as it billowed out.

"Chief! Fire on the rear wall, crawling up toward the ceiling. Spray the roof!" Davis radioed in his observations from the inside.

"Nicholas, you heard him! Blast the roof!" I turn the key and push the button for the high-power spray to cover the roof and hopefully keep it from spreading. It will be a while before we get this under control, and I'll lose a day of interacting with the public. I'll need to make up for it, but I wasn't worried about her getting ahead of me. She shouldn't even be a blip on the radar.

I wasted my time pulling that prank.

Sometime later:

"Alright, shut it off, wrap it up, and let's go home." Chief radios. My arms are sore, and my ass is numb from sitting for..." I check my watch; it's after 1:30 a.m. I know I'm going to pass out at the firehouse. I can't even make it home.

What looked like a simple fire was complicated by the unauthorized storage of flammable materials. It fed the flames, though luckily, none of it ignited. We had to stay and fill out the police report. They are definitely going to get a hefty fine.

Once we got to the station, I barely had the energy to shower, but I was sweaty. I pull off everything, and my phone buzzes. It had been doing that all night, but I ignored it while battling the blaze. Now, I was too exhausted to care. I put it on my bed and ran in for a quick shower.

A few hours later:

"Nick, wake up! Nick!" I'm jolted by someone nudging me.

"Wha-what?!" I looked over to see everyone gathered around me. I ran to the mirror because I could be short an eyebrow or have a permanent marker handlebar mustache, courtesy of my buddies. Seeing none, I walk back and sit down groggily. Davis struggled to stop snickering, and a laugh slipped every time he made eye contact with me.

"What is it? Cause I'd like to go back to sleep."

Beckham also looked like he was struggling to keep a straight face. "Umm...Kelly got a hint that she should stop by your house last night, and...it's different."

"What do you mean different? Wait, did someone break in or vandalize it?"

He shook his head, "I think you...you should definitely go home and see." I don't know why they were smiling, but it didn't sound funny.

I didn't even blink; I threw on some clothes, grabbed my phone, and drove like a bat outta hell. Now I have to call the police, log the damage and what's missing, and get a new security...what the hell?!"

My tires screeched by how hard I stopped. Perhaps it was because my snowmen were decked out in sexy lingerie. There were bra sets, slips, and chemises, solid and lacy, red, black, and any other color that would stand out against the white figures.

The desecration of my snow figures...that's not the worst part...no, it's the giant sign that read, "SANTA NICK SAYS COME AND GET IT, BOYS!"

Now I know why my phone was constantly buzzing. I see phone calls, voicemails, and numerous text messages. Some with people taking pictures with the lingerie-laced snowmen.

"ELIVIA!" I scream at the top of my lungs before I go visit my naughty neighbor.

~

Elivia

BANG BANG BANG

The hard knocking startled me and had my heart racing. I realized I had fallen asleep downstairs. I open the door and yawn simultaneously, but it doesn't shield me from an angry-looking Nick. Or at least he was until his eyes took in my outfit. I was still in my costume and doing that stretch you automatically do while yawning, further tightening the already stretchy, skin-tight fabric across my body.

"Well, well, well, what do we have here?" He leans forward, resting his muscular forearms against the door frame, towering over me. "Is this Elivia, the mischievous evil elf costume? How... appropriate." His eyes travel south, and I follow; the zipper is lower than before I went to sleep, and now it sits under the swell of my breasts. I chose to leave it, fantasizing about him slamming my body against his, taking control as he slid the zipper down painfully slow before I ended up bare in front of his hungry stare.

"So, tell me...are we even now? Because, although drop-dead gorgeous, you're still a nobody in this town, and you're not going to win." I swear I heard a distinct growl. It complemented his bedhead and the skin-tight grey Henley he was wearing. He was either trying to intimidate or seduce me; I couldn't tell.

Wait...did he call me a...

"A nobody?! Well, be ready to kiss this nobody's ass when I win!" I kiss my fingertips and turn to tap my backside to give him a visual.

"Ha! Fat chance. I'm going to dismantle your pathetic little display."

"I want all my lingerie back!" I scream as he walks away confidently, closing the door quickly. It was freezing!

∾

Nick

"I WANT ALL MY LINGERIE BACK!" She screamed as I walked away. I stopped in front of the display with sexy thoughts in my head, knowing every piece of fabric caressed her body. I could warm my house with my body heat the way she riled me up. After she slammed her door, I pulled the pieces off, carrying them all in my hand. I could have gone over there, but I went inside and did the unthinkable...I sniffed them. They smell like her, floral and sweet with a hint of seduction. She could have sprayed them to distract me. She knew...knew I'd perv and smell them.

Why would a woman own so much lingerie? I mean she did work for the company, maybe she gets a big discount. I take them upstairs and toss them on the bed.

Would I return them? Eventually.

But first, I needed to relieve the throbbing; I couldn't go back over there with a hard-on. I wanted to stroke myself to an explosive orgasm with every thump. I grabbed my catalog and lay on my bed. If only she could watch me like I ogle her. I hadn't even made my first move, but I will! For now, I had endless pages of this beautiful blonde. Both she and Elivia rile me up to no end. I found myself only looking at this woman. Yes, the other models were pretty but unmatched to her. This was a double winter holiday issue, and she was wearing every character of Christmas. I saw her in the Mrs. Claus' outfit, just as sexy as Elivia's. I turned a few pages and saw the elf costume she was wearing earlier...I stopped stroking...because...

I turned on my table light because I needed a good look at her face. In this picture, she was in a blue lingerie set perched on top of one of those incline things that help with sex positions. I don't know the correct title; it was a sex pillow. She was decked out in makeup that mirrored the icy blue set. I flipped to a more natural photo, her in a split front red negligee, her hand behind her head, pushing her hair away from her face. I'm not sure if Elivia realized with her deep plunge elf costume that I got a glimpse of an outline of a tattoo. The heart had some writing on it, but that sexy, stretchy fabric kept part of it hidden.

Only part, but make no mistake...

"Holy shit, it's her!" I know that mischievous smile, gaze, and those beautiful long legs, but that tattoo confirmed everything! After learning I was a few feet from the woman I often jerked off to, I resumed playing. A literal supermodel lives next door. How interesting. Well, I still needed to get rid of my current situation.

10

ELIVIA

I spent the day at the shop and the night doing the same meet-and-greet routine; the crowds were smaller as we got closer to the town celebration where they'd announce the winner. I was beginning to suspect that my repeat customers had an ulterior motive, and I guessed right! In fact, it got me three date offers from his company alone, but I would never go out with any of them. The spark wasn't there like it was with Nick.

Thinking back, when did I become so vicious? Where I couldn't take a simple prank and became so cutthroat. I need to fix it but also have a little fun. When I ordered supplies, I ordered a five-foot tree for my bedroom window that needed decoration, and I knew he'd try to see what I was up to.

There's nothing wrong with teasing, right?

I see his lights on the main floor; he hasn't made it upstairs yet. I took that time to wear my Mrs. Claus costume, tease my hair, and put on my favorite red lipstick. No boots this time because nothing is sexy about falling off a ladder. I'm setting up the tree and centering it in front of the big window when I see the light go off downstairs.

Let the fun begin...

Nick

THE CROWD WAS SMALL TODAY, and I focused on them, not my sexy neighbor next door. After a long night, I sat in my recliner with my beer and Santa top open, exposing my bare chest and beard on the side table. I chug the last of it before turning off the lights and heading upstairs.

I slip off the Santa jacket and set it over the chair on my way to wash my face and brush my teeth. I stop before my window, contemplating whether to take a look. It was a quick peek; besides, she probably wasn't in her room, which would wrap up my day.

I step forward and am pleasantly surprised. She put up a small tree in her window. She was decorating it and dancing around...in that Mrs. Claus outfit.

I found myself in a dream world where I would sneak up from behind and wrap my arms around. She would squeal to let her go, but I would only toss her on the bed and eye her like a predator does his prey before I fulfill all the things she begs me to do to her.

I can't deny this unbelievable attraction towards her even though there has been some...tension, I will not give up without trying.

I stand shamelessly in front of the window again. I needed to know what would happen if she saw me boldly standing here. I watch her practically perform a strip tease while decorating the tree, but then she stops when she sees me. Her gaze causes me to run my hand down my chest and abs. She does nothing besides staring into my soul. I can feel my body temperature rise, and I lean forward with my arms against the window, getting a closer peek, and she smiles. She waves at me, and as much as I want to wave back, I want to seduce her more, so I wink and lick my lips.

She traced her body with her hands, caressing and teasing me as she reached for an ornament. She stood on her tiptoes to place the bauble near the top. She tiptoed back, making her breasts bounce deliciously. From what I could see, she only had part of it decorated; perhaps that show was for me. I lean back and clap before returning to my predator stance. She walked forward, grabbed another, the same color, and held it up as if asking for my opinion. I shook my head no. So, she pulled the box back a bit, stepped in front of it, bent over and

"Sweet Santa, baby!"

And I didn't mean the song because I saw a flash of her cheeky red lace boy shorts. She turns around with her hand over her mouth, mouthing, "Oops." Well played, Elivia, because if I wasn't hard before, I definitely was now. I wasn't bold enough to show her, but I did rub myself like last time as I watched her continue to decorate the tree. First, she would step up on the ladder to place the ornaments; she reached down seductively, not bending her legs with a skirt that barely covered her. I prayed for the skirt to give way, but fate was not on my side. She stretched the lights and placed them behind her before plugging them in. The illumination against her skin was mouthwatering. She swung her hips as the bulbs followed her motions. I imagine the sexiest slow music playing to accompany this holiday striptease. She brought them around like a blanket to illuminate her delicious breasts. She unwound them from her curves and quickly slipped them between her legs, pretending to slide them against her pussy and sending pleasure through her body.

This is the hottest thing I've ever seen. Then, she placed them around the tree. She was almost done, bending down for the star topper, and pressing it against her luscious lips. After blessing the star with her steamy kiss, she stands on her tiptoes and places it gently before turning her attention to me.

I was still standing like a predator, but I shifted and ran my hand down my chest. I saw her lick her lips before she turned away from me. She looked over her shoulder as I saw her arms move, but I couldn't figure out what she was doing...

Until she turned around and revealed that Mrs. Claus's costume had a center zipper that she had unzipped to reveal a red bustier with matching boy shorts, she let the dress fall to the floor. At that moment, I wondered if anyone else in the neighborhood could see her like this. She didn't seem to mind or care, but I did. Predators are territorial, and if she is interested in me, I won't hesitate to let the world know that I will be the only one unwrapping her Christmas box.

All this teasing had me shot up like a firehose on full blast, and I waited for permission. I bite my fist as I stare at her while she watches me. I have to adjust; it's too much. I pull the velvet pants tight to mold against my dick. The satin lining on the inside feels like soft torture and glides against me as I shift him to the left. I see her lick her lips, and then she gestures for me to come over. A simple flick of her finger for me to 'come here' and I did not hesitate to throw on my top but leave it unbuttoned. I was ablaze in lust; not even a blizzard could calm down this inferno. I slip on my boots and grab my keys.

11

ELIVIA

His gaze is liquid sex, and I don't know what's come over me when I unzip to reveal one of my favorite lingerie sets and get so bold as to invite him over. Maybe it was his molten stare or his sexy rippling muscles, but we know it was the imprint of his dick when he shifted it.

He's supposed to be my sworn enemy, my competitive rival, my arrogant, cranky neighbor who called me a nobody! But I also wanted to feel him inside, against, and all over me. He disappeared so quickly that I only had enough time to wrap my black robe around me before I went to the door.

I knew... I knew. There was no knock, but I sensed he was there...waiting.

I exhaled while opening the door, and he rushed forward so fast, grabbing me by my neck and stepping forward enough for him to slam the door.

I gasped at how rough he was, how dominant, how controlling. He pushed me until I felt the chill of the wall on my back. "Now, who told you to cover up?" He impatiently peeled the robe off of me, tossing it to the side, and then his grip tightened, further cutting off my blood flow but not my breathing. I felt tingly all over. If he had pulled my hair, I would have melted. The intensity of his stare caused me to whimper. "Nick…"

"Baaaaby," He growled, "damn, you sound so carnal, so goddamned needy for me." His finger traced my pouty red lips while his hand came from around the back of my neck to the front and slowly down the center, making sure he groped my tits before sliding further down. Thoughts of him slamming into me while gripping a little tighter dance in my head.

We locked eyes, my breath labored in anticipation, "Please…"

"Please, what? Hmm? What do you want Santa to do to you?" His hand inching ever lower. I feel the heat of his fingers sliding closer. None of this made sense. I should be trying to get to know him to see if we should get to this point, but I couldn't take the back-and-forth competitiveness and constant teasing. I took the risk, and now I have a very sexually aggressive man about to take what he wants from me and give me every orgasm I'm screaming for.

He leans in closer, and I can smell him. It's the signature masculine scent, and after many nights of bar hopping or attending high-end social events, I know Tom Ford's Tobacco Vanille when I smell it. It's one of those scents that make your mouth water, among other things. It's a sensuous blend of tobacco leaf, vanilla, and ginger. Warm & spicy.

I want to smell him on my sheets long after he's gone tomorrow. To wrap my naked body in the essence of him.

Teetering on the edge, I grab his wrist to tell him to stop teasing me, but that's not what came out!

"Do anything you want. Please." I mewl, anticipating our first kiss.

He leans closer, a whisper away, "Are you sure? Because I won't control myself once you submit to me completely, Elivia." He growls my name, adding to the intensity of this situation.

"Yes..." In that instant, I saw his resolve break. I feel his breath on my lips, awaiting that moment of satisfaction...

Beep beep! Beep beep!

"FUCK!" He shouts out aggressively. He reaches for his waistband and pulls out his beeper. I feel the internal blaze extinguish quickly as I lean against the wall disappointedly. He looks at me, trying to figure out what to say.

"Go. I get it." I said dejectedly.

He surprises me with a rough but sensual kiss; his tongue slips in and torments me so recklessly that it rekindles my fire and leaves me screaming for more.

"I'll be back, beautiful. Don't you even think about touching yourself until I come back." He sweeps his fingers across my underwear and watches me shudder almost violently, "This... belongs to me. I'm going to devour you. Nobody or nothing else, understand?" He pulls my hair, and my knees buckle in lust.

"Yes, sir." He pulls me forward enough for him to reach around and smack my ass hard with one more fire-inducing kiss. "Good girl." And he races back over to respond to whatever emergency just came up.

I bit my lip as I slid down the wall until my knees touched, overwhelmed, and surprised by his dominance. Contemplating what happened, I have never said 'yes, sir' that way my whole life, but when he punctuated his demand with such force, I knew that's what he wanted to hear.

I hear him quickly pull out of his driveway while I'm a pulsing mess on the floor. I don't think anything, but him could extinguish this burning desire. My brain hit replay of the last moments and conjured scenarios of what could happen upon his return.

I glance at the clock on the wall. It was late, would I wait up? Keep the door unlocked so he can walk in. It may not be NYC, but it was a dangerous risk. Maybe I'll wait a while and leave a note when I go to bed. I went to the kitchen to fix a cup of cocoa. The snowfall was heavier, fatter, and quicker to make landfall. Perhaps this was the winter storm I had hoped for.

Nick

I'D NEVER HATED ANSWERING a call until that very moment. My dominant side is highly agitated, pissed, and horny. Well, the last one was us as a collective. In my costume, I run into the firehouse and see everyone not getting into gear or rushing toward the engine.

What in the ever-loving fuck?!

"Hey, look at sexy Santa with his chest out! Did you greet your visitors like that? I bet you earned all the female votes tonight. Not a bad strategy; sex sells." Beck says nonchalantly as he nudges me.

"No. Why were we called? I thought there was an emergency?"

"Ohhh... yeah, Chief wanted us all at the station in case this storm got bad. Reduces the chances of being stuck at home and unable to answer calls. We have to check and plow the driveway and road every four hours. Kelly was so pissed! We were...busy in the shower..."

I tuned out because I was in a situation of my own that I was mentally repeating over and over.

"Nick!" Beck yelled, and it triggered me.

"What?!" I snapped, catching him and a few guys off guard. He didn't answer quickly enough, so I angrily stomped to my locker to apparently set up my bunk for the night, mumbling curses along the way.

I had her. I fucking had her, only a hair away from devouring my fantasy girl. I won't lie and say that the moment I walked into my house, I didn't smell her sweetness on my fingertips and then taste her.

Now, I want more. I need more.

She's graced the cover for millions to see, and I almost had her submitting to me; she wanted me...it made me so...

"Fuck!" I angrily slam my locker. I rub my face as Beck waits for me to respond. I groan before leaning against my locker. "I'm sorry, I'm a bit...pent up. I had her, Beck, so close to falling apart."

By my literal fingertips!

"Who? Ohhh...Elivia? I thought she hated your guts after your little failed prank. She ripped you a new one when we stopped by. Although a siren like that could be a real animal in bed." He scratched his chin. "But maybe there IS something there. I know Jackson, Perry, and I think Thomas gave it a go, and she turned them all down. Sounds like she won't turn you down."

She didn't.

The territorial me is not pleased to know that they went behind my back to try to nab a date with her. They spread the rumor about her interest in me, but I suppose since I hadn't made a move, they thought she was fair game.

She's not.

"Well, guess I won't find out anytime soon, huh? And look, we're definitely getting a blizzard tonight. If I had her number, I could tell her not to wait up."

"I think she'll know. You better not let another chance pass you by next time. I heard Xavier at the shop opening. He was definitely vying for time with her. He gave her a rose before he walked out; while we were walking in, I saw the last moments of their conversation, so you're on borrowed time, buddy."

"Thanks," I said bluntly. I remember that she held onto that flower while we were talking. He had earned bonus points because women love flowers.

"I'm curious, Nick. How would you feel if she won the contest? This competition has been basically your mission since you decided to recommit. Can you be okay with not winning? Would or could this affect how you feel about her?"

"I still want to win it...to honor them and their love. I'm not going to back down because of my feelings, that's for sure. She's still my competition and the only one that's got me by the balls," I admit.

"HA! Quite literally, you might want to uhh...get rid of that."

I look down, and now I have a red tent, pitched and ready to go. "Bloody hell...you got to cover for me. We weren't even called in for a real emergency, but this is! Give me two hours." I'm begging my best friend.

"If I cover, you have to take my next two shoveling shifts."

At that moment, a pulse shoots through, causing me to relent. "Fine, deal. I gotta go!"

"Don't you want to put on some clothes?!"

I'm still a blazing inferno. It doesn't matter if old man Winter stood beside me; I'd melt him into a puddle. I had an itch I needed to scratch.

12

ELIVIA

I was sipping on cocoa that was gifted to me from work. Of course, it wasn't regular store-brand cocoa. No, it was Tiffany's brand cocoa in its signature robin egg blue packaging. I hate to admit it, but it tasted richer and smoother. Perhaps the French/Belgium blend chocolate excused the $100 price tag. It's currently the only decadence I can indulge in since I'm not supposed to satisfy my own... urges. I watch the snow fall gracefully as it builds and builds. I left Angellica a message saying not to go in tomorrow. The music playing is slow and sensual. My light touch along my neck reignites the fire between my legs.

I sigh long and hard, "Fuck me." Then, I sipped my sweet concoction. It is sinfully delicious. I took a few more sips before retiring to bed. Every moment awake reminds me of our intense interaction with no happy ending per se. I stand to stretch, feeling the smooth silk rubbing against my hardened nipples. I rub my hands against them, and it feels so good I can't help but sigh and moan at the same time. It was unbearable. I had to do something to calm my nerves or the incessant pulsing of my pussy that demanded to be filled to the brim.

How would he know anyway?

I made up my mind to help myself. I was so riled up that I wouldn't reach my bedroom without bursting into flames. I lay across the couch nearest the front window and sighed in relief as my hand slipped up to my breast, palming and squeezing, enjoying the warmth of cupping them. I shudder as my entire body is covered in goosebumps. I run my fingertips from my knees to the bottom of my underwear; it sends shivers up my spine. "Mmm..." I pinch my nipple, fantasizing he was here commanding me to get on my knees and hold my tongue out. I would work him into a frenzy until he couldn't take it anymore; what I wouldn't give to hold that tiny bit of power over him until his knees buckled.

I was so lost in the moment until I heard a knock. I barely had time to fix myself but opened the door anyway. Nick stops mere centimeters from our bodies colliding. I gasped and peered down; he was sporting quite a hard-on.

"Tsk, tsk, tsk..." He walks around me, "What a sight to be had when I peered through the window to see a disobedient little girl touching herself. Didn't I tell you not to touch? I'm afraid you just landed on Santa's naughty list."

I might be on the naughty list, but judging by his erection, Santa's been thinking inappropriate thoughts.

His fingertips lift my chin. "You must be punished for your misbehaving, yes? Maybe then you'll get back on my good side?" He turns me and smacks my ass so hard, but I refrain from making a sound. That intrigued him.

"Upstairs. Now."

I had never moved so fast in my life. I could hear the heavy footsteps of his boots slowly following me up the stairs. I stood in the center of my room, shaking in anticipation, awaiting his presence.

It's taking longer than I expected. I felt like prey, but prey that wanted to be devoured. I cross my legs to dull the sensation but instead intensify the pulsing. He's torturing me by making me wait. I heard a couple of thuds before he rounded the door, without his coat, barefoot, and only in his Santa pants.

He momentarily leaned against the doorway before approaching me quickly, wrapping his hand around my throat. "I have less than two hours before I have to report back, but it'll be two hours you never forget. Now..." He roughly snatches my robe away and pulls down my bustier, exposing my breasts without any barrier. If we didn't have a time restraint, I'd enjoy watching him undo every hook from the eye, slowly baring me to him. I'm almost lost in thought until he brings me closer to him, a hair away from another deliciously sensual kiss. He doesn't oblige, further teasing me, "Tell me, Mrs. Claus, were you going to deliberately disobey and bring pleasure upon yourself when I specifically told you that this sweet pussy was mine?"

"I..." He shushed me.

"I didn't ask you for a response."

But you did. I keep my lips shut, trying not to be a smart ass.

Nick

SHE HAD a smart-ass remark on the tip of those smug lips, but she would find out that I was running the show tonight.

"On the bed, Mrs. Claus." She looked over her shoulder with a hunger in her eye. It was silent defiance, and I responded with my hand on her ass, hard and fast, then squeezing her cheeks.

"Even your silence is disrespectful. We'll fix that eventually, isn't that right?"

She slid her entire body across the bed, laying on her stomach with her feet in the air. "Yes, Santa." She purred.

I stood behind her, taking in the sexiest mental picture. I put one knee on the bed...then the other. And now, I'm straddling the small of her back. Her body shuddered before I even touched her.

"Don't you dare think about looking back."

I rub my hands together before I start rubbing her back. Her skin was soft and smooth like she had just gotten out of the shower...or tub, where she punished herself to the thoughts of me repeatedly taking her. I lean down to kiss her shoulder and across to the other shoulder and feel her body relax as she sighs.

"Such beautiful skin...you smell like dessert, and I always make room for dessert."

She shifts around to face me. I pinch her nipples as punishment for disobeying me. She squirmed and moaned, indicating pleasure from it. I was going to make her want me. I don't think I have to try too hard.

I lean in closer, pinning her hands above her head. Now, I had to connect her wanting lips with mine. Her breathing was labored, causing her breasts to bounce. I was going to kiss her passionately, almost violently. Abusing her lips, leaving her lipstick smeared, her lips more swollen and to the brink of orgasm.

I glanced at the clock; I only had an hour and a half. I wanted to enjoy her all night, but this stupid snowstorm and my obligation to the station limited my time. Plus, I didn't want to risk getting snowed in; I mean, I did because what better way to enjoy a snowstorm than naked and snuggled up in blankets and body heat? But I didn't want to face the wrath of the Chief as to why I wasn't where I was supposed to be.

But at this moment, I am the luckiest man in town, claiming my supermodel neighbor.

"Nick..." She whispered as her hands ran down my chest. I slam my lips against hers and finally feel her fingernails scratch my back and her legs wrap around me. "Patience, Princess." Her lips curled upward before she flipped and straddled me, putting my hands above my head.

WHOA!

She rocks herself against me, and I can feel how ready she is for me. I allow her to take control for a moment.

"But you said you only have a little time, and I need it... rubbing against you...ugh...feels so good."

She was correct; she slid her pussy back and forth against my hard dick. If I lost control, grabbed her hips, and sped up, I'd leave a mess on my chest. I needed to feel the most intimate parts of her. I shift to lay on my side and pull her against me. One arm across her chest while my hand wandered slowly down. I kissed her from shoulder to neck while tweaking her nipples, causing her to purr. She pushed her ass against me, trying to get her relief. My hand slid between us, using the tip to stroke her slowly from the back while my fingers teased the front. I grunt as I slowly envelop myself in her. Her squeals and moans drive me to pump faster and harder.

"Mmm, Nick!" My name never sounded so perfect.

"Elivia, baby. You feel amazing." I growled in her ear, and I swear she tightened even more.

Fuck!

Screw work. I wanted to pound into her until the sun rose, but I knew I couldn't. I would see how many orgasms I could gift her before Santa had to return to the North Pole.

"Oh! Right there, don't stop! I'm gonna..." She grunted before her entire body shuddered over me and tightened her walls. "Ohhh!" She exhaled, but I kept going, pounding her pussy for my own orgasm.

"Oh yeah, you're Santa's good girl, aren't you? Fuck, you feel so good, baby." My thrusts faster, and her moans egg me on to give her another orgasm while chasing my own.

She was soaking wet. I switched positions, kneeling, watching myself sliding in and out while holding one leg against me for leverage.

"Oh God, yes! It's d-deeper, so much deeper." Damn right, I was bottoming out against her but not like a jackhammer. Feeling her pulsating walls had me teetering on the edge, but I wanted to come together. I lick my thumb and circle her clit. She gasped as she sat up on her elbows to watch me. She grabbed her tits, squeezing her nipples as she licked her lips. I leaned down to take those, too.

I slide out, and she whimpers until I position her on her hands and knees, taking her deeply from behind with my hand wrapped in her hair, pulling tightly from the root. It was my favorite position to finish.

"I want to hear it, Elivia. I want Mrs. Clause to scream my name."

"Nick!"

Wrong. I smacked her ass and slowed my thrusting down. I hear her whimper, needy for her satisfaction. "Want to try again?"

"Umm, oh, Santa?" She was guessing, earning her another smack, but she seemed to enjoy it this time, so I stopped altogether.

"Last chance, I have to get back soon, and I'd hate for Mrs. Claus not to get her Christmas present."

I slowly start back up, and her walls react to the friction, and she does too by rocking back against me. The countermotion sped up the freight train that was this orgasm. I only gripped her hips tighter to slam her against me.

"Oh, St. Nick!"

Bingo.

"Say it again."

She's panting hard and super close. I slow down to prolong it a little longer. I lean close to her ear, pulling her hair to meet me halfway. "Say. It. Again. Then you can cum. I can feel your greedy little pussy wanting to release and quiver all over me. One more time, for Santa. Only good girls get presents."

I flip her on her back again so she can feel me deep in her when I slide in. I slipped out to quickly devour her when I realized I hadn't tasted her essence since teasing her before I had to report in. She was soaking wet and tasted so sweet. I wanted to taste her during the rest of my shift tonight.

To Hell with milk and cookies.

I feel her hand in my hair, pulling roughly, responding to how amazing she must feel as I lick my plate clean. I look up, and she's still panting, trying to decide if she wants to grip my hair or the sheets. I changed my mind and decided to taste her orgasm all over me instead. I resumed licking, swirling, and teasing her. Her cries get louder, her grip tighter, and I can feel her start to shake.

"I'm...gonna cum...fuck me!"

In due time, Elivia. Santa wants to finish his snack.

I lightly stroke her while continuing to devour my meal.

"Cum for me, Elivia. Give me a very Merry Christmas." She tried to roll her eyes sarcastically, but instead, they rolled into the back of her head when I focused on her button, and she shattered like a dam bursting. Her body buckled, and she locked me between her legs until she returned from her blissful state. She looked at me without a word. I smirk as I swipe her sensitive pussy lips to taste her once more as I line up against her.

I watch her intensely as I slide in; her tightness is almost unbearable but so wet and ready for me. She squeezed against me as she gasped. Every waking moment, I'll be thinking about the feeling of her against me. That primal urge to claim her by slamming into her to hear her scream set in, and she did not disappoint.

"When there's more time, I will claim every inch of this body. Do you hear me? You, this pussy...is mine. Fuck, I'm gonna cum and fill you with my holiday spirit." I growled out my orgasm, pumping a few more times because she felt so damn good. I look down at her eyes closed. I check and see that she's breathing. Did she pass out?

The pleasure must have been too much, and as much as I want to pull her against me and go to sleep, I have to return to the firehouse.

I'll get her fireplace going so the downstairs won't be frigid in the morning. I kissed her temple and shoulder. She turned over and mumbled something in her sleep. I pulled the cover over her naked body and took one last peek.

"Goodnight, beautiful. Remember that you're mine."

I grabbed the pieces of my costume, lit the fireplace, and ran to my house for a quick change to not hear Beck's stupid Santa jokes upon my return. The snow didn't seem to be piling up at the earlier rate; it had lightened up quite a bit. Maybe this wasn't the big storm it was predicted to be.

Either way, nothing could get me down. I finally claimed my neighbor.

13

ELIVIA

I woke up and realized I was completely naked. That only happens when...

Then I flash back to last night and blush all over. I spent the night with Nick! Ooh, he was so dominating yet so gentle. He was the perfect mix of a Southern gentleman who loved to satisfy my needs and a bad boy who knew what he wanted to do to me.

I pull my sheets up to inhale his scent that, sure enough, lingered between the threads. I lay there for ten more minutes until Mother Nature called. I stood and stretched as I looked out the window at a few inches of snow. I know he wasn't home, but if he were, he would have had a bird's eye view of my nakedness before I went to stand under the hot water.

I know it happened, but I still can't believe it. He was so... deliciously rough, but behind it was a gentleness and eagerness to please me. I wrapped myself in my fuzzy, warm robe to counteract the impending chill downstairs. I was pleasantly surprised to feel the warmth and see the fireplace lit.

He lit it before he left. There's that gentlemanly side.

The chill on my feet counteracted the nicely heated room. I see that we didn't get the amount of snow we were expecting. Perhaps I'll go in and do inventory.

Nick

I WALKED in a new man and didn't feel bad when the Chief saw me stroll in.

"Sorry, Chief, last-minute business before we started shifts."

"I expect you to take the next shoveling shift in 15 minutes." He checks his watch.

"Sure, Chief, not a problem." I salute him before walking away.

I head to my locker while being watched by a few. I could see Beck turning down the heat on the giant pot on the stove. It could be soup or chili. Either way, I worked up quite an appetite.

"Well, aren't you in a better mood? I take it you don't mind taking my shifts plus the next one?"

"The way I'm feeling, I will take every shift. Nothing can get me down. You won't believe..."

Before I could explain why the alarms went off.

"Alarms triggered at the high school. Damn, kids! This better not be the senior prank. Let's go!" Chief bellowed.

These kids are going to get coal in their stockings. At least I get out of the shoveling.

The snowfall was light, almost endlessly floating around as the wind blew. The engine sirens come roaring alive as Davis takes the wheel and starts rolling it down the driveway. It's our duty to run and catch it before he makes the turn onto the main road. It's a test of testosterone and endurance. Having a company full of men, we make everything a contest.

I was the first to make it onto the truck. I think it was because I was a few quarts lower and thus quicker.

Beckham barely makes it before Davis makes the turn onto the main road. He's panting hard as he tightens up his uniform.

It's too early for kids to be at school, at least not for another hour and a half. Shit, this could be the senior prank.

When we arrive, smoke is billowing out of the back door of the cafeteria.

We noticed a couple of cars in the parking lot, "It's the lunchroom! Clear the staff!"

Beck, Jackson, and I donned our masks while entering the smokey building. We can hear coughing from the kitchen behind the double doors. We quickly make our way through the cafeteria.

"Hello?! Asher Falls Fire Department!"

There is no answer, just the coughing, which lets us know they've been there a while. Any longer, and they'll asphyxiate.

"I see the source!" Jackson yells as he disappears to contain or put out the source. I walked towards the coughing, which was becoming less and less noticeable.

"Asher Falls Fire Department!"

Gasp "Here!" ***Cough cough*** "Over here!"

I hear them struggling to get air into their lungs; the smoke reaches the floor, so the air is almost nonexistent. I slid my boot around until I felt something, and then a hand grabbed my leg. I reached down, threw the person over my shoulder, and back-tracked to the exit.

"Call the ambulance! We got casualties!" I set them down and recognized Miss Doris. She was my lunch lady when I was in school.

"Miss Doris, can you hear me?"

Her eyes opened and fluttered wildly before she gave me a slow thumbs-up.

"Give me the oxygen, stat!" I immediately put the mask over

her mouth and nose and coached her to breathe slowly and deeply.

"Miss Doris, who else is here?"

Before she could answer, Beck came out with Mr. Floyd, the grill master.

Davis comes running with another oxygen tank. Mr. Floyd grabs it and takes a deep breath of fresh oxygen, making him cough hard.

"Is that everyone?" Davis asked while donning his mask in case he had to go back in. I could hear the fire extinguisher going off; the smoke billowing was now stark white.

"It was only Floyd and me. We were getting breakfast started early to make our famous breakfast burritos. We always come before dawn when we make them."

"I remember those. They were always the best. Keep breathing slow and deep. You too, Mr. Floyd. I know you want to breathe deep and fast, but that causes more harm than good. Nice and slow." He slows down his rhythm to match hers.

I grab another extinguisher and go back in. Davis had to have used the entire thing by now.

"Davis?!"

"I'm by the window." I saw the windows open, and the smoke being pulled out, improving the view a bit.

"What's the cause?"

He points at the griddle. "The bacon grease overflowed the reservoir, and some went down this metal cord into the outlet. It did a bit of damage to the wall but nothing to shut down the school. They'll have to replace the stove, though. I think this stove is as old as the school because of the metal cords. Definitely out of regs."

"That sucks. Remember how excited we were for breakfast burrito day? It signaled how close we were to the holiday break."

"Is that what they were doing? Oh man, those were the best. It was tradition." Sadly, these kids will miss out on such a core memory.

"Hey, maybe we can bring the portable griddle from the firehouse and do something like pancakes?"

"We have those big containers of pancake mix in the pantry, and maybe someone can grab more bacon and some syrup?"

"Yeah, let's do that. Let's keep the windows open and gather outside with the plan."

As the Chief writes the report, we tell him the plan. "So, of the entire company, how many men do you need for this?"

"Davis and I can bring the griddle and mix in the pickup. Beck and Jackson can grab some bacon. The rest can man the station for any emergencies."

Chief looks around at the damage. "Alright, that's fine. That's a nice thing you're doing for the kids." He pats my shoulder before walking back to his truck.

Miss Doris grabs my hand, "You don't have to do that."

"I know that, but we want to. Let the paramedics look at you, and if they clear you, you can start on whatever batter you have here. Prepare it and set out the butter."

I can see the tears well in her eyes, "Bless you, Nick."

"You remember me?"

"Are you kidding me? You are a carbon copy of your parents. I went to school with them, you know? They were in love from the beginning, and everyone knew they were forever. And you are the product of that forever love."

I saw the twinkle in her eyes when she mentioned them. "Thank you, Miss Doris. The paramedics are here to check on you. We'll be right back."

With our assignments, we take the engine back to the firehouse and split off to salvage the school's breakfast tradition.

After grabbing the griddle, several containers of pancake

mix, and spatulas, we head back to the school. We connected the griddle inside but cooked right outside of the door. We split the griddle for pancakes and bacon. I handled the bacon while Davis was the pancake stacking master. He can pile them on like no one else. He can cook at least eight at a time. Beck and Jackson plated them, and Miss Doris and Mr. Floyd served them to the students. You can see the damage on the siding, plus the fire department was here helping out and I think they understood why they were missing out on the breakfast burritos. However, these pancakes were the size of dinner plates and super fluffy. Every kid seemed content and thanked them and that's enough for us.

Three hours later, we pulled up to the coffee shop. "Dude, I am exhausted and smell like syrup," Jackson says when he sniffs his shirt, wiping off the sweat from his face.

"Yeah, but the kids enjoyed them. Making them massive was a great idea."

"Two words: Football players. They could easily scarf down three plate-sized pancakes. Did you guys eat like that back in high school?"

I pointed, "Becks did. He was the quintessential football jock."

He tried to look shocked, as if we didn't attend school together. "I was not."

"Dude, you played football, baseball, and rugby. And homecoming king and…"

He slapped his hand over my mouth, "Alright! Change the subject. You didn't spill the deets."

He didn't need to go further; I knew what he meant. I keep the door open as the guys walk in.

I need a vat of espresso stat!

"What's up, Xavier! Can you make four travelers of the extra bold roast?"

He nodded, "Yeah, it's gonna take a few minutes."

Beck and I slide down to a table by the pickup to chat.

"You were damn near skipping when you came in. Is it safe to say that you bagged Elivia?"

"How crass. I wouldn't say that; I would say I've claimed her, and that's not the best part. You've seen her before."

His brow raised, and he sat back, "What do you mean?"

"I mean, you've seen Elivia before. In a magazine the firehouse subscribes to, a certain catalog showcasing sexy risqué clothing for women..." I trail off while watching him try to put two and two together. I see Xav topping off two travelers while preparing the other two.

"Well, it isn't Penthouse or Playboy because we don't subscribe to those. They also don't sell clothing. Let's see, the only thing other than that is the Sugar Sweet catalog we ogle."

Now that I think about it, I dislike that they were ogling who was now my girl.

"Wait, are you saying she's in the catalog? Elivia is a Sugar Sweet model?" He said a little louder than I was expecting, but everyone was in their own conversation by the order line.

I nod, "Yup. I didn't know until I saw a very discreet tattoo confirming it. You'd have to be pretty close to even know it was there."

"Discreet, huh? Dude, that's fucking awesome! You're banging a model. Maybe you can convince her to bow out gracefully so you can win the contest!"

"What, no? I can win fair and square; no need to do anything drastic."

I see Xav close to us again; it looks like he was finishing off the last traveler while we waited at the counter.

"I feel bad for leaving her after the fact, but as soon as we are cleared to go home, I'll be right back there. Me, her, and the fireplace."

"Dude, you don't have a fireplace."

"No, but she does." We share a laugh as we grab the containers. "Thanks, Xav."

"No, thank you."

Wonder what that meant?

14

ELIVIA

It wasn't a snow-laden winter wonderland like I had hoped. I wore my flat snow boots with simple leggings and a tunic sweater. I was going in to take inventory and work on the books. The store would still be closed, so dressing up was unnecessary.

Honestly, I'd rather be lying naked under Nick.

The thought of it has me overstimulated. I needed to take my mind off last night and do something productive. Or I'd start planning our lives together. I didn't even know if this was an itch he scratched or if he was truly interested in me. Knowing that he knows me just for me makes me hopeful.

I started the whimsical music to keep me in the holiday spirit, humming to my favorite tunes.

It only took me two hours to balance and double-check the books and sales. I went into the office and sent the report to corporate with a note of how amazing this place is and a special note about how awesome Angellica was.

Then, I walked around the store, taking inventory before I went to lunch. We were running low on silk chemises and lace underwear, and we had sold all the beginner bondage sets. My town had a bunch of closeted kinky people, and I loved it. I guess I could order the more provocative type of stuff you see in adult shops and see how they react.

Knock knock

I look up to see Xavier at the door. He is handsomely dressed in all black again. He was overdressed, but color me curious.

"Good afternoon, beautiful." He held out his hand and I placed mine on his. He lifts it to kiss my hand and I can feel the blush on my cheeks.

"Afternoon, sir," I reply coyly.

"I came by to finish what I started at the grand opening. I wanted to take you to a movie and get to know you."

I opened my mouth, but nothing came out.

He smirks, "Perhaps I can sweeten the deal with this." He presents me with a long stem red rose from behind his back."

"Oh, thank you. That's so sweet of you."

"I'll always try...for you." He's laying it on thick and I'm trying to keep my boundary lines drawn. Especially now that Nick and I have become intimate. I mean, I suppose we could still go as friends.

"Xavier, can I take a rain check? I've got a lot going on right now. Can we hang out after the competition?" I was trying to avoid words like date.

"That's fair. Know I voted for you."

"Trying to earn bonus points? Well played."

He takes a business card and scribbles down what I assume is his number, and then he kisses it.

"Whenever you're ready." He winks before leaving.

I head to the grocery store to grab a few more supplies before I head home. I decided I was going to leave a note for Nick to come light my fire...er, fireplace.

∽

Nick

THE ANTICIPATED SNOWSTORM WAS A FLOP. Mr. Cunningham holds his hands up, "Sorry folks, a rogue warm front cut our promising front and essentially shredded any chances of decent snow. We did get enough to enhance those gorgeous contest entries vying for the grand prize. So, don't forget to get your vote in for people's choice." I suppose that's a good thing; hopefully, we get released from duty soon.

I daydreamed about the good times with my parents when my mom teased me.

"*Nicky,*" The only person allowed to call me that. "*I want to see you settled down and happy. You have your father's charm; any woman would be lucky enough to have you.*"

"*Oh really? What about Tracy? She obviously didn't think I was good enough.*" This was right after she broke up with me, and I was wallowing in self-pity on mom's couch after a five-day, no-movement stint in my apartment. She threatened to "tar my hide" if I didn't come home. After telling me I looked like a hobo, she made me shower and wash my hair.

"*Her?! Hmph, she was a two-bit hooker with bad manners. I wouldn't want that swamp donkey in my family anyway.*"

I roared up, laughing so hard I had tears from it and not from the heartache. I never heard her talk ill of anyone. I'm sure she whispered her insults to my dad, but I had never heard them until now.

"*Mom!*"

"*If you would have told me she was joining our family, I would have disowned you. Honey, I'll never make decisions for you; you are meant to figure life out, the good and the bad. I am here to nurture and love you through all of it.*"

She kissed my forehead and patted my hand, "*When you find the one, you'll know, and maybe one day someone will call me Nana...or Glam Ma since I'm so fabulous.*"

I never gave her that chance, and I know she's up there telling me it's okay, but the remorse will always be there.

Then, my mind shifts to Elivia and our night together. I didn't know what this was, but I could hear my mom's voice, "Try," and that's what I'll do.

"Alright, hose bags, you're free to go except shift B; you'll start your shift today."

"Come on, Chief, can't we take credit for yesterday, coming in early?!" Perry screeched from the 2nd floor. "Nice try. Shift starts in an hour." All the B Shifters groaned loudly. Thank goodness I was shift A.

"Just for that, you can start pulling out the decorations and supplies for the holiday party!" An even louder set of groans echoes the walls. I quickly pack up my stuff to head home.

The snowfall was super light but still visible. What I wouldn't give for an unexpected polar front to come through in a few days, but not now; today was the last day for the people's choice voting. After that, they would take the remaining days to count the votes and declare the winner at the holiday festival.

I see the warm glow from her house. She'll be outside in God knows what, but I know she'll be mouth-wateringly sexy. I stuck with my Santa costume because who doesn't love Santa? Her lights turn on as soon as I park in my driveway, and I see the flutter of her curtains.

Tease.

I grab my laundry bag and get ready to open my door when I see a piece of paper wedged in it.

Milk and cookies after the showdown. My place. A roaring fire would set the mood perfectly, please... Santa?

Why can I hear it in a low and sultry tone? It sends shivers down my spine, especially begging Santa to light her fireplace for ambiance. I shake myself like a dog before stepping inside. I put cookies in the oven and head upstairs for a steaming hot, then ice-cold shower. Santa can't show up with a stiff one, especially on the last day when the undecided come by for last looks. This time more discriminating and looking for evidence of flaws. Maybe I need a second tray of cookies?

The shower did nothing to fan the flames, but it kept me from going full mast. Before closing up the coat, I shove the pillow in front, which keeps him at bay and against my torso. I played sexy Santa most of the time. This time, I wanted to look like the jolly Kris Kringle the children knew and loved. I'm sure I got a lot of the single votes; now it was time to bribe the children because in Santa's bag was full of toys and candy. A little bribery never hurt anyone. I had to remember my bottom line was to win this for my parents.

I played the family's rendition of the 12 Days of Christmas to hone in on those sweet holiday memories. As expected, the masses came around the winner's circle, as they call it, for one last judging glance. I lay it on thick this time.

"HO HO HO! Merrrrrrrry Christmaaaaaaasssss! Season's Greetings from the Nicholas family. Come and get a gift from Santa, kids!" Once I said that, some kids changed direction entirely to get a free gift.

"Thank you, Santa!" They chime with big smiles while holding a toy, candy, and a cookie in their hands. With every handful, I felt a vote my way.

Then I hear the sound of bells and automatically look in her direction. I had to keep my jaw from dropping as she pranced out dressed as Rudolph the red-nosed reindeer, a sexier version with a skin-tight suit and antlers and a shiny red nose. She wore brown knee high boots and a harness.

She's distracted by the visitors; I set the bag and cookies down and walk behind her line of sight.

15

ELIVIA

I chose Rudolph to end the voting round. I'm sure I bagged most of my votes as sexy Mrs. Santa. That's also when I bagged the big man himself. He wouldn't respond to my note until after this last effort.

"Merry Christmas, everyone! Make sure to vote for me before I return Santa to the North Pole."

"Will you help Santa come to my house?" A cute little girl in a blue puffer coat and white knit hat with pom poms asked me.

"Of course. Have you been a good girl?" She nods enthusiastically. "Then I'll make sure he comes by your house; make sure you vote for your favorite reindeer." She waves after taking a warm peanut butter cookie. I see her look back at the sign. Thank goodness our houses were numbered by the committee for easy remembering.

I made sure to interact with everyone who toured my display. I knew, even though I wasn't paying him any mind, that he'd been watching me since I pranced outside. The bells on my leather collar, bracelets, and ankles were a dead giveaway.

Growl

"Don't even think about turning around. Keep smiling and

handing out your cookies. Santa looks forward to drowning in your milk and eating your cookies later." Then he inhaled deeply and continued to growl as I tried to remain welcoming when all I wanted was to be in a sea of endless orgasms.

"H-hi, welcome to my home. Please take a l-look around and enjoy a cookie from Santa's favorite reindeer. Isn't that right, Santa?" Nick had no choice but to nod his head in agreement. Santa wouldn't lie to kids, would he? I laugh at my small victory over him.

He put his hand on my waist, squeezing, "Well played, Elivia. You'll pay for that later."

I can't concentrate with him behind me! I tried to regain my composure and some power by rubbing against him. He couldn't feel much with the padding, but it was still a tease.

"Teasing Santa, huh? He's got a special gift for you to unwrap, but only if you do what Santa says." There was no one at either display, so he made his move. His hand, which was on my waist, slid down the thin fabric. I think I knew what he was looking for. He slid his hand down from the middle of my side until he quickly squeezed my ass.

"Hmm, Santa didn't feel any panty lines. Good girls don't do that..."

I smirked and wiggled a bit, "I know."

I felt a sting and yelped at the burning, tingling, yet satisfying pain of his hand on my ass. "You'll be spending all night working *on* Santa's workshop."

"Wait, don't you mean *in* Santa's workshop?"

He gives me a knowing look, and I clasp my hands in front of me and sway left and right, and then I give wide, innocent eyes. "Yes, Santa." I knew he'd like that.

"Good girl. I'll be over one hour after the official close. No touching, teasing, or getting off. I won't be so lenient this time."

Ooh, is that a threat? I nod because I'm already a soaking wet mess. "Yes, sir." Another deep guttural growl. He steps away, walking backward, watching me. I bounce on my heels until I see some people coming my way.

Nick

WHY DOES her every movement rile me up to no end?! Watching her tits bounce was almost my tipping point to throw her over my shoulder.

Soon, Nick, soon.

As soon as time was up, I didn't even look her way; I headed inside to clean up. I took the hottest shower I could tolerate, so she would have to work for it. I had to think unsexy thoughts... she would earn her ride on my sleigh.

There were some wayward flakes falling, but nothing that signaled a significant amount. It's that perpetual snowfall from what accumulates on the nearby mountains that the winds pick up, and we were almost completely surrounded by mountain ranges. I'm still hopeful for a surprise. I think I've been a good boy this Christmas.

I walked out of the bathroom in my towel to see if she was in her room preparing for me, but it was dark. I rub my hair as dry as I can and toss it and the body towel in the hamper. I look over to see movement in the curtains and chuckle. She got a free preview before I put on my gray jogger suit and heavy-duty boots.

I thought about bringing a bag, but I had no shame in doing the morning-after stroll.

I stood at her door and listened briefly to see if I could catch her running down the stairs. Hearing nothing, I casually lean against the door and knock.

I guess I should have brought something, like a bottle of liquor since I already gifted her wine. Before I could think about turning around, the door opened, and she grabbed and yanked me in. The door slams, and I'm against it with her against me. Her lips fervently on mine as my hands immediately wandered. But I was met with the smooth feeling of silk. My curiosity got the best of me as I separated, "Someone's eager." She smiles as I take in her outfit, if you call it that. It consisted of a silk robe, and I'm not sure of much else; she had it wrapped tightly. The fact I could see her nipples led me to believe she was completely naked underneath.

Merry Christmas to me, indeed.

Then I noticed she layered blankets on the floor beside the fireplace. There was food and drinks on the table beside it.

"I didn't know if you'd be hungry, so I made snacks. There's wine and vodka. I have tequila, too, if you want."

I was hungry, but not for food. "Didn't take you for a hard liquor girl."

"I'm more rational knocking back shots of liquor than a glass of wine. Wine makes me... want to hump things." She blushed so hard it resembled Rudolph's nose.

"Wine it is, then!" I headed toward the kitchen, but she pulled me back. "Nick..." I wrap my arms around her. "Oh, alright. I'll have a vodka and orange juice, please. You make it, and I'll start a roaring fire." I tap under her ass to feel her soft skin, confirming she is naked. Fuck me. I set up the woodpile and lit the fire. I stare at it for a while, enjoying the crackling sounds before I place the fireplace screen in front.

I felt the chill of glass on my shoulder. "Thank you for lighting it." She plops down on the blanket bed, which loosens her robe; she's about to pop out. It's turned into a deep V-neck plunge almost to her belly button, teasing me with her skin, especially that cute little heart tattoo. I sit on my knees, pulling off my shoes and sweatshirt, pulling my sweats down to my hip for a sneak peek. I catch her biting her lip.

"What's with the bed of blankets, huh?" I shuffle behind

her, placing my hands on her shoulders, rubbing and massaging. She takes back a shot; judging by the color, that looks like tequila.

"It's part of my holiday fantasy."

"Oh...was screwing Santa on there as well? To have a not-so-silent night?" I slid the loosened fabric off her shoulder, but she didn't move. It pooled at her elbow, almost exposing her breast.

"Not until about a week ago." Then she looks back, and her gaze incinerates me. She looks ahead at the flames dancing on the logs. I lean down and kiss her shoulder, and she sighs. I pause to down my glass. It doesn't matter what I drink; I become an animal. Besides, I wasn't going to let her outdrink me. As it goes down my throat, I realize how strong mine was. It was a double vodka and orange juice.

Clever, clever girl.

"How about some holiday music to cap off this fantasy?" I asked. She reached for a remote and tuned into one of those 24-hour channels. The smooth voice of Frank Sinatra belting the classics filled the room.

"Good?" She asked. I take that moment to slide the fabric off her other shoulder, revealing her beautiful breasts. "Now it is."

I sit back and pull her between my legs as I palm them. Her hands cover mine.

"Nick..." She whispered.

"Santa." I corrected her.

"Ok, no. Listen, I can't be moaning and screaming 'Oh, Santa Claus,' it's weird."

"I'm the hot mall Santa, and you didn't seem to mind last time."

"To be fair, I was teetering. I would have agreed to anything."

I take note as my hand goes between her breasts and down

her stomach to tease her relentlessly. Rubbing circles on her stomach before lightly digging my nails into her hip, causing her to jump. Her breathing picked up as I continued. "Good to know because I'm going to enjoy playing with your...ornaments." She keeps trying to wriggle away, so my other arm holds her steady against my chest.

When I slipped between her legs, I was surprised at how ready she was. I bring my fingers to my lips and watch her watch me taste her.

"Much better than milk and cookies."

She was so taken aback by the boldness of my actions. She retaliated when she reached behind her back to squeeze me playfully. I almost jumped but then enjoyed her squeezing in a pulsing pattern as she stroked up and down.

Then she turns around to straddle me and forces me to lean back on my forearms. With the fireplace roaring, her hair sexily strewn about, and me shirtless, it was the perfect book cover shot.

I would have stated that had she not shoved her tongue down my throat. Feeling her rubbing up against me is torture.

"I need you...I want you. Take me now, please."

I raise my brow, "Please, who?"

"Oh, come on, can we not?"

I push her robe to the side, circling my thumb on her clit with a cocky smirk, "But darling', it's the holidays. Why not spice it up? Besides, it drives me wild when you cum screaming out, 'Oh, St. Nick!'"

"It was one time." She panted, trying not to show how it was affecting her. She couldn't concentrate on anything but.

I latched onto her nipple, nibbling lightly while stroking her softly.

"Didn't you black out in extreme pleasure?"

Her leg started to shake, "Wh-what happens after the holidays, and you can no longer use those corny Christmas lines?"

She smiles arrogantly. I know they were cheesy; they were meant to be. A girl loves a funny guy.

I bite harder and she whines, "We'll worry about it then. Santa has a long night away from Mrs. Claus on Christmas Eve and only wants to hear one thing. Can you give me that?"

She didn't notice I held her up while releasing myself from my sweats. I was devouring her breasts; she put her hands in my hair and pulled. I let her lift my head up and she locked eyes. Then she glanced over and pointed. "Look!"

There was quite a steady flow of snow out there and it was pretty windy. I see the gleam in her eyes. I might actually get snowed in with this beauty.

"It's perfect!" She squealed, and I took that distraction to slam her down on me. She gasped, clasping her hand over her mouth.

I grunted, "Now it's perfect. Sweet Santa baby, you're even fucking tighter." There was no slow and steady; it was a furious pump to feel her squeeze against me, getting wetter with every thrust. She matched my thrusts with her bouncing and...ohhhh...

Don't cum, don't cum, do not cum!

Even though I'm trying not to paint her walls, I also don't want her to stop. "That's it...faster, Elivia. Take your Christmas present from me. You earned it for being such a good fucking girl!" Then she switched from bouncing to rocking against me, and it was so much better. Fuck! I gotta last at least past her orgasm.

"Nick! Ohhhh...mmm!" I grab her by the neck and bring her lips to mine. She pulls back, rocking even harder, "So...fuck-ing...good...soooo good." I swear she's purring as she's quiv-ering all over me.

"Be Santa's good girl and come all over my cock, all over my lap, until your legs give out. Give it to me, 'Livia."

She slowed down, "Is that what you want...Santa?" Then she

let me slip out. I took advantage and positioned myself behind her. She dropped her top half, and the angle was dangerous. Every angle has a different feeling, different pressure against you, and if that dorsal vein gets enough friction...

I felt the tingling warning me to finish her before I did. The way her ass bounced back and the force of it was hypnotic.

"I'm gonna cum! Keep...going. There, there! Oh, St. Nick... fuuuuuck!" See? She didn't need any coaxing from me at all.

"Oh, baby!" I never had a chance. I fall away from smothering her to end up on my back. Then I feel a fuzzy blanket cover me and hear her giggle.

I'm trying to catch my breath, "What's so funny?" I throw the blanket back off and she bites her lip at my still-hardened state.

"Cool your jets, princess. It'll go away when I calm down. I've had quite a workout." I stated arrogantly.

She wraps herself up in her portion of the blanket before lying against me. Now, we face the fireplace with a prime view of the snow falling. I can't see her face, but she keeps bumping against me, letting me know she's still awake or wants another round.

"Nick?"

"Hmm?"

"Tell me the story about your parents."

"I'm sure you've heard it already."

"I did, but I want to hear it from your view. The only person who can truly tell the depth of their love for each other. They sound like my perfect Hallmark romance."

"They definitely were. Let's see, they were high school sweethearts. When they graduated, they went to the University of Pennsylvania and started living a simple life together. Mom said Dad was a total slob and a nightmare the first few years, but she used her 'ways' to fix him. I believe it evolved to that mom look that she used on me because mom had a look that could kill if you didn't do what you were told. I...I certainly miss it." I caught myself and looked out the window. I felt her hand brush my cheek but refrained from looking down at her.

"Anyway, after college, they moved here because they always knew they wanted the small-town life. Mom was a librarian, and Dad worked at the welding plant about 30 miles from here. One day, I asked him why he didn't move us to that town. He looked at my mom and said, 'Your mother loves her job and this town; why would I uproot her from her happiness? I'll gladly sacrifice for her and you.'"

16

ELIVIA

Oh, my goodness, his father was so in love with his mother, and I'm swooning. "Your dad sounds like Prince Charming himself."

"He was, every single day they were together. Even when they had a dispute, it was never that serious. I knew it was settled when there were fresh flowers on the kitchen table, or they were outside dancing to no music."

Are you kidding me?! Their love is worthy of a romance novel.

"When I was a teenager, they decided to enter the town's Christmas decorating contest. It was going to be our family tradition. The first few years, we didn't place. We didn't start placing until I was in my 20s. My dad said he had been silently observing all these years. We started winning second place, then third the next year, but when we finally won, I had never seen my mom so proud! Our winning photo was the Christmas card for the next year. Those next few years were the best..."

Nick exhaled hard, taking a pause to gather himself. I continue to rub my thumb against his cheek as he places his hand on my hip.

"You don't have to keep going. I know it still hurts."

"No, it's okay. It's always going to cause pain in my heart, but I heal better when I remember that the good will always outweigh the bad. It feels good to tell someone finally and they don't look at me with pity in their eyes."

"I can't guarantee I won't make that face, but I want to listen." He faces me away so he can wrap his arms around me.

"I know. Back then, I didn't want anyone's pity. I wanted to know why he would take both of them from me at the same time. I cursed his name and prayed for him to take me too. Their love for each other was what made me. After a week of no contact, Beckham broke my door down, and my entire company was there. They cleaned my house, cleaned me up, and fed me. They covered my shifts and took turns checking in on me. I was such a wreck that I never cried after their funeral. I bottled it up and turned it into anger. I projected it on all things having to do with Christmas. I purposefully used blackout curtains and minimal lights; it was seasonal depression amplified. Looking back, I was teetering, and it could have gone south fast had they not intervened."

"I couldn't imagine that amount of grief. Thank goodness you're still here. I can see why the competition is so important to you." Then I felt his lips on my shoulder. "So, what about your parents?"

A subject I didn't want to delve into, but I suppose since he revealed such a personal part of himself.

"There's no everlasting love like your parents. Mom was a nurse and dad was a firefighter. He met her when he got pinned down at a factory. She was the first face he saw when he regained consciousness."

"A firefighter, huh? I can see the appeal." I feel the laughter in his chest. I didn't reciprocate; I think he sensed it when he kissed my hand.

"They had a solid year together before he was killed in a gas explosion on the upper East side of Chicago. My mom found out she was pregnant the day she saw them wheel in his body to the ER. I am the only living memory of him." I sigh, trying to collect myself. "Around five years old, my mom met my stepdad and they've been together ever since. He's a great stepfather, but I wish I had met my real father. I have a whole album of them together. I see the resemblance between him and me. I am his spitting image, and I know that it breaks my mom's heart. She never said it, but I know she wishes she knew sooner so that morning before he left, she could relay the good news."

Next thing I know, he's nuzzling into my neck with kisses, and I hold his arm with my hands.

"I'm so sorry, darlin'. The positive thing is that from them came you. I bet your mom's eyes shine when she sees what their love created and he's watching you every day."

"Well, I hope not right now. That'd be traumatizing."

"What, that his baby girl was having sex?"

"That and playing into this little holiday kink you seem to have."

"It's not the only kink. Besides, I was playing off the season, and you didn't help with all those sexy holiday-themed costumes. Seems like this was right up your alley."

He was right. I couldn't say I got these from Sweet Sugar; he could put two and two together. I didn't reply. I grabbed my pillow, wedged it under my head, and lay in comfortable silence until I heard him snore. I knew there had to be a flaw in there somewhere. It wasn't subtle, either. This was one of those bone-tired, finally getting some sleep after a week of 12-hour shifts type, snores. I suppose that makes sense, being a first responder and all.

I wasn't tired, so I slipped away and put on my robe to fix myself a cup of decadent cocoa. The snow was collecting nicely in the yards but not the roads; the pavement was too warm—probably another disappointment.

Nick laid on his back, pushed the blanket down to his hips, and put his arm behind his head. He looked like he was finally getting some much-needed rest. I stared at his home and the significance of his display. How could someone not fall in love with their story? This was his town, and these people were his family, especially with how they took care of him after his parents died.

I couldn't take that from him. It was rightfully his to regain. I decided then and there to cast my vote for him and drop out of the competition.

"'Livi...'" I see him shift back to his side, asking for me as his hand reaches and doesn't feel me there. He doesn't wake up, so I finish my cup and resume being under him. His body seemed to relax once my skin pressed against his.

It may only be a few days away, but Merry Christmas to me.

I woke up to a very brightly lit room and remembered that I slept downstairs and then the rest of my memory kicked in. I looked over to see Nick wasn't there. Maybe he's in the shower? I didn't see him in the kitchen. I walked upstairs but didn't hear the shower running and he wasn't in my bed.

"Huh." I went back downstairs to fix breakfast; judging by the still-clear streets, Angellica and I were reporting to work. I texted her to be in at normal hours and that I'd bring coffee.

His truck is gone, but there's a note near the coffee maker:
Sorry, called into work. I'll make it up to you. Dinner? -Nick

Dinner is a nice start, but I won't forgive him until after he devours me until I can't breathe.

I head upstairs to take a shower. I'd grab a bite at the cafe.

I parked at the coffee shop, and Angellica texted that the store was super busy, more than usual, and that I should hurry! Wonder what that was all about? Probably last-minute shoppers, it never fails.

I hurried into the shop. No one was there besides Xavier. He greeted me with a smirk, "Good morning, princess. What can I prepare for you?"

"Two double shot macchiatos, two blueberry muffins, and two bananas."

"That's a lot of food."

"It's for me and Angellica, she said it's packed in the shop. Must be the last-minute gift buyers."

"Or the fact that we have a bona fide supermodel in our midst..."

My stomach literally dropped. "Wh-what? What did you say?"

"Well, yeah. I overheard Nick when they were here about him banging some supermodel from Sweet Sugar. It wasn't hard to figure it out with just the two of you. Angellica is a pretty girl, but she's nothing compared to you. And to be honest, Nick was very cocky and arrogant about it. I would never brag like that about you, especially to a group of pigs."

I swear Xavier's words sounded like an echo. All I could think about was how long had he known? Was this before or after we slept together? The first time? Last night? Was I a notch in his belt that he could brag about to his caveman friends? I was red hot!

I broke out of my daze when his hand flashed past my face, "Elivia? You zoned out there. Are you okay?"

"Tell me everything you heard." I hear the weight of my emotions make my voice crack.

"Well, Beck asked if he had bagged you yet and Nick was like, yeah, man and to top it off, she's a supermodel from Sweet Sugar. All those times we've been whacking it to our subscription, I'm the only one to nail her. Then Beck said he could probably convince you to drop out of the competition, especially if you were screwed good enough."

I literally gagged and put my hand over my mouth. How could he say such vile things? And tell everyone?! Did it mean nothing? I felt the tears prick my eyes but refused to let them fall. I took refuge in the nearest chair and Xav handed me a water bottle.

"I'm so sorry. Maybe you shouldn't go in."

"I never wanted anyone to know about my past! I left New York to start over and now....argh! That dirty son of a bitch!" I texted Angellica, letting her know I was going to drop her breakfast off before running a critical errand. Maybe Xavier heard wrong, that this was a misunderstanding of biblical proportions. For Nick's sake, it better be.

"Can you cut the order in half? I'm suddenly not hungry."

"Sure." He rubbed my hand, "He's not your only option, Elivia. I don't care about what you did in New York City. I care about getting to know the girl who walked in and took my breath away. Undoubtedly the most beautiful girl in town and I want to know her better, not because you graced the cover of magazines. You deserve to be with a guy who appreciates you for you and not for bragging rights like a college frat boy douchebag. Especially after how he spoke about you like you were another piece of ass. You deserve better."

I hear his words, but my thoughts are so loud I can't give him my attention. I'm pissed and upset, embarrassed, and disappointed with myself. I didn't even notice that he left, prepared my order, and brought it over to me.

"Here. No charge."

I shook my head, "No, I can't let you do that."

"It's fine. Think of it as a friend helping a friend."

"Okay, thank you." I couldn't get over Nick's gloating. All I wanted was to find someone to be happy with before they knew about my past. There were too many who only dated me for status to say they dated a model. It was so superficial and fake, so I left New York. I guess I was wrong to think I could hide it or run away.

When I got to the store, it was busy. I walked in and was

instantly bombarded. "Miss Winters, can I get your autograph? It's so cool to have a model live here! I just want to say you are so pretty and can I have a selfie?" I was so numb when everyone left that I locked myself in my office to cry. While I don't mind signing and taking pictures, it demoralizes me to feel like an object; it's emotionally draining. My life is a wreck after the most beautiful night with someone who I thought cared about me.

Then I hear little taps, "Open the door."

"I'm fine, Angellica."

"You're obviously not! Now open this door; don't keep this bottled up." I relent while sniffling. She hugs me so tight. She loosens up but doesn't let go until I chuckle.

I'm met with her sweet, cheery disposition. "How about a girl's night? We can watch bad horror movies, drink lots of alcohol and complain about men. You can invite Kelly! It can be a total bitchfest! I need to vent about my ex, anyway. He keeps leaving flowers at my door."

"Sounds like he's sorry and trying to make it up to you."

"Then he shouldn't have knocked up my sister!" She screeched and then gained her composure.

"Come on, we deserve to vent."

"You're right. Take this hundred and grab supplies, then go to my house and set up. I need to say my piece. You can close up early; I'll do the books in the morning."

Before I knew it, I was heading to the firehouse in my car. I didn't know what I was going to say, but it was going to be unfiltered.

I was noticed before I even made it up the driveway. I recognized some of the guys when they came by my display and the few who got the balls to ask me out. There are a lot more in his company than I expected. Some were working on equipment and a couple were in the kitchen, but Nick was nowhere to be found.

A blonde-haired guy approaches me with a wide smile. "Elivia?" He had a creepy look as he eyed me up and down. "Nice to see you again."

I raised my brow as a nonverbal cue to tell me who the hell he was, not that I cared.

"I'm Perry. Remember, I tried to ask you out?" He held out his hand, but I glared at him.

Ugh, I don't have time for this. I wanted to make sure my anger was directed to the right person, but his partner was about to get an earful if he didn't get out of my face!

"Where is Nick?" I said rather loudly as I walked around him. I see him lounging in a recliner, sipping a beer completely shirtless.

Beckham got his attention and pointed in my direction. He stood up and was only in his fire uniform pants, the suspenders at the side and I could see the top of his boxers. I wanted to run my fingernails down his broad chest. Maybe they had to run drills. He smiled as he approached me. "To what do I owe this wonderful visit? Did you miss..."

Smack

I didn't know what I would do, but that felt right. Every person visibly gasped and turned away.

"Livia?"

"Don't you dare call me that, you bastard! You look me in the face right now and tell me you didn't know about my previous job at Sweet Sugar and then bragged about it like some arrogant asshole!"

Everyone quickly scattered to other parts of the firehouse. He still looked shocked until his shoulders slumped, "Yeah, I figured it out when I... saw your tattoo when you were in your elf costume. I matched it up to the catalog with the Grinch outfit, but I never bragged about it, I swear!"

I remember that. They had me zip the costume to my belly

button to showcase the matching shelf bra and garter set. I thought they airbrushed it out.

"Who did you tell Nick? I'm sure the whole crew here knows because men love to brag about their latest conquest!"

"What? No, I...I only spoke with Beck about us."

"Then how did Xavier know and was able to repeat back what you said word for word, huh?! He said you bragged to Beck about 'banging a supermodel', is that it? Was that the only reason you slept with me? To add to your body count? Do you know how that makes me feel?"

Not only did he freeze, but I saw Beck gasp in my peripheral vision. No doubt it was true.

"Baby, no, it's not like that."

He reached for my hand, but I snatched it away. "Don't. That job gave me nothing but heartbreak full of arrogant, pompous men who used me for status. I was tired of it, Nick. I wanted to come here and find something genuine. For someone to get to know me, just me. I was starting to think I had found that in you. I don't know what's worse, that I was so quick to trust you or to sleep with you. The blame is on me, but don't worry, I won't make that same mistake again."

I quickly turned away because I felt the build-up of frustration and tears about to fall and I wouldn't give him the satisfaction of seeing how hurt I was.

17

NICK

What just happened? I mean, what the hell?! I could only watch her storm off to her car. She tried to hide the heartbreak in her eyes, but I saw them fill to the brim before she turned away. I really mucked this up until I realized what she said.

Everyone was trying to busy themselves while I stood exactly where she had left me. I run my fingers through my hair until the anger surfaces.

"Xavier...that son of a bitch was eavesdropping and twisted my words. I'm going to put my fist down his throat! That lying coward!"

I was going to have a friendly visit, but Beck stood in front of me with his hands out. "Whoa, whoa, whoa! Don't do that. It's what he wants, to make you look bad in her eyes."

"I'm already the goddamned bad guy! Now I'm going to rearrange his fucking face!" I lunged forward, but he stopped me again. I know he was trying to get me to calm down, but it only pissed me off more. "I didn't know she was trying to remove herself from her old profession, Beck. It was never a factor before or after I found out; it was just a part of her. I

would never use her for status or count her as a number."
Angrily, I swung all my frustration at the punching bag in the
corner where the gym was.

Beck followed me, "You have got to let her calm down
before you try to do anything. You don't know how to do that,
so, let's continue this impromptu gym session to burn off that
energy." He stands behind the bag to give it more stability.

I hate to admit it, but he was right. I had no idea how to fix
this, but I knew one thing.

This was not over.

~

Elivia

I WAS in no mood to socialize, but Angellica called Kelly and
invited her over. "I was already coming by after talking to my
knuckle-dragging ape of a Neanderthal husband. I'm so sorry,
Livi. Be there in 15 with provisions." That's woman code for
chocolate and liquor. I could definitely use both.

While Angellica put together some food, I dismantled the
blanket bed and threw them in the washer, adding too much
detergent. I didn't even want his scent in my house. I'd also have
to wash my bed sheets, which made me even angrier. All the
pain was confined to my house because I'd never been in his
home.

It fell on me, as always.

Every candle lit, I tossed it and threw the grate in front of
the fireplace.

"Hey, change into some pajamas. It's a sleepover." Angellica gives me a hug before I go upstairs. Then I thought
about all the lingerie I wore during whatever this was.
Luckily, I remembered the red and green striped set my
mom got me. It was a button-down, tank, and pants. Far

from my usual, but that's fine with me; I wanted no reminder.

I gave myself a small smile in the mirror. I'm impressed by my mom's pick, minus those gaudy earrings. She has pretty good taste. I take a few minutes to will my social butterfly to cooperate because my girls are here for me.

When I come down, Kelly is here, and they are both in their warm, fuzzy PJs.

"Aww, sweetie. It'll be okay. Let's, umm, pop some popcorn, bring the board to the table, and I'll make alcoholic hot chocolate. How does that sound?"

I wanted to say it sounded amazing, but I could only squeak out an okay. Close to tears again, they surrounded me in a hug before sending me to the couch and handing me the remote to pick the first movie.

Unfortunately, my television was plotting against my heart as the notable Hallmark channel logo glowed in the corner of the featured movie, Love *for the Holidays,* and what was next? *Stealing Santa's Kisses.*

"Oh, Christmas cock-sucking hell!" I screamed. They both looked at me, shocked. To be fair, I was impressed with myself for making my insults holiday themed. It also reminded me of all his cute holiday colloquialisms, and I'm emotionally back to square one.

I quickly found the Horror Network. One of my favorites was about to start. Thank heavens.

It was starting to get dark, and I saw the lights and displays starting to come on around the neighborhood, so I promptly shut the curtains. I look up to see them observing me.

"Alright, missy, before we venture into what happened, I wanted to let you know that Beck told me Nick isn't taking this well. This is not to justify what he may have done but to know that this is more than a fling to him. Now, tell us what happened. Here's your tipsy hot chocolate to help."

It was super strong, but it helped me dive into my feelings. The next thing I know, I'm in tears laughing, listening to Angellica's story about her awful ex. She holds her hands up, "Then he shows up to my job pleading on his knees. I told him I'd forgive him if he stripped down naked. So, he did, what a dumbass. I was recording the whole time. Then I tossed his clothes out the fourth-floor window! He had to go back out butt naked and everyone had their cameras out because I told them my plan and shortly after that, I quit and applied for this position when it was advertised. As for my sister, the entire family disowned her. She moved to Montana or somewhere. It was my lowest point, but I knew I deserved better."

"Wow, Angel. But you're such a sweet person. I would never think you would retaliate like that!"

"Circumstances define what version of me you see."

I look at Kelly, "Remind me never to piss her off!"

"Me either!"

Then a scream came from the movie, causing Angellica to jump, scream, and have popcorn fly everywhere.

It was momentarily hilarious, then I sighed, "What am I going to do? Part of me says it's stupid to be mad that he found out. Anybody could have, but the other part questions the authenticity of everything he's done. Am I crazy?"

Kelly pops a grape in, "Crazy, no, hopeful, yes. I know you wanted an FBI-level type disappearance like witness protection, but sweetie, all you did was change your hair. You're still that beautiful girl with a luminous smile. You cut your hair shorter, that's it. I know you've had past bad experiences with them using you for status and you're going to take what we say with a grain of salt, but do not cut ties. It's okay to step back and think."

I look over and see Angel nodding in agreement. "Hey, are you going to turn on your display? It's dark outside now."

"I dropped out of the competition. I was going to tell him

that I voted for him for the viewer's choice." I hugged my pillow and looked away.

"Oh, Livi. That's so sweet of you."

"Yeah, well, now I feel like a fool. I don't even want to celebrate my favorite time of the year...because of him."

"Okay, enough about men unless we're watching someone lop off their head. I vote for the Nightmare on Elm Street series. Angel?"

Angellica pushes up her glasses, pondering, "Good choice, but I'm thinking Final Destination. Playing on your worst fears. Livi, it's your house, your decision."

There was no question in my head; it was the furthest from holiday cheer. "Ladies, I need something intense, and nothing screams it better than the Saw franchise." They both nod and grab more food. I'm thankful for them because I would have made a knee-jerk reaction when I needed to think this through.

18

NICK

Because of the incident between Elivia and me and my discovery about Xavier, the Chief banned me from any coffee runs during my shift, which started today. They're keeping him alive for the short term, but I was going to get my hands on him one way or another. Beck promised to keep me informed through Kelly if I went straight home. I never bragged about us. I was lucky, even fortunate she was even talking to me. Why would someone so beautiful want such a regular guy? She could be on the arms of celebrities, sports athletes, or other models, but she chose the quiet life and found interest in me. She would never be a notch on my belt. It was an insult; she meant so much more.

I drove home in silence, and my heart dropped when I turned on my street. Her display wasn't on. She looked as dark and desolate as I did when I was mourning. In a way, she was mourning the possibility of us. I wanted to go over there and explain, but there were two other cars, and I know one was Kelly's. She'd rip me a new one before she allowed me to even look at Elivia.

I wanted to try and start over, to ask her to be my date for the holiday party and the town festival. I had less of a role at the company party since I asked the Chief to swap me out as Santa because I could no longer bring goodness and cheer to the children. He agreed and then swapped me and Beck. Now, I was his dorky elf sidekick.

I contemplated turning my lights on or keeping them off. I could hear fond memories of my family's singing and decided to switch them on. Plus, I wanted her to know that I was home on the off chance she might sneak away to talk to me. I would be okay if she came over to scream at me as long as I was in her presence.

I could only hope.

I did all my usual after-work tasks. I was so thankful the interaction portion of the competition was over. I couldn't bear to see the hurt on her face as we tried to put on an act for everyone.

Now, it was getting around town what she wanted to keep tucked away, and even though Xavier twisted my words vindictively, it was my fault. I told Beck, and telling even one person betrayed her trust. I didn't even stay downstairs. I went and watched her window and drank a beer. Of course, the lights were on downstairs, and judging by the time, they were definitely going to make a night of it.

Knock knock

I never moved so fast to get to my door.

"Eliv...oh." I turn around and down my beer in disappointment. Beck comes in with his duffle and sets it down.

"Want a beer?"

"After the ass chewing I got from the missus. I need a double shot of Jack in addition to the beer. Since I'm in the doghouse, I thought I could use some company." I set down two shot glasses, a bottle, and two beers.

I see him look around, "How are you holding up?"

"I'm fucking miserable because of what Xav said to her. Why would he..."

"Don't be blind, Nick. He wants Elivia, probably since their first interaction. Then he gifted her the rose at the store opening and kissed her hand while in super close proximity to her. You were worried about Perry and the guys in our company when your competition has been sneaking in from the sidelines. When he overheard our conversation, he took that info to strike a fatal blow between your relationship or whatever it was."

I growled, "She's mine."

"You might think that, but nobody knows you two are together or dating. Technically, she's still fair game until you make your intentions known."

I groaned and wiped my face, "For fuck's sake."

"Yeah. So instead of spying on her from your bedroom window like a creeper, let's watch a movie and brainstorm."

"How did you know what I was doing?"

"I heard you coming down the stairs like a freight train, and your light is on up there with it being dark down here. Come on, stalker."

I guess I wasn't being as inconspicuous as I thought.

Everyone would be at the firehouse tomorrow, and then I would start my plan to make her a permanent fixture in my life.

A thought popped up, "Beck, I need you to convince Kelly to bring Elivia to the firehouse."

"Oh, so I got to die for your plan to work? I told you I'm in the doghouse. She's been extra emotional lately, too. This little incident caused a complete meltdown."

"You're playing Santa; you can present her one of her gifts, make it a grand romantic gesture with flowers and a heartfelt note."

He scratched his chin, "You might be on to something. I did get her a Tiffany set to celebrate our upcoming anniversary. We can get a card tomorrow; in the meantime, do you have a notepad? What I have to say won't fit in a card."

We started on our plan because, after today, I have nothing more to lose.

Elivia

THE SLEEPOVER WAS JUST what I needed. I got to eat junk food and drink an ungodly amount of liquor. We swapped laughable, absurd stories about men and the dumb things they did. Then I swooned, listening to how Kelly met Tyler. He's been going by his last name for so long she chuckles every time she calls him that. "When I'm boiling hot, I call him by his entire name, Tyler Jeffrey Beckham, and he heard that earlier for his part in all this mess."

"I didn't mean to get him in trouble."

"He's not in trouble. I was disappointed in his use of language and objectifying women. He's never spoken like that in front of me, and to hear the things he said was so disappointing. I think it was my hormones because..." She paused and looked away, wiping a tear from her eye. "What if we have a daughter, and she meets a man who talks about her like that? I'm sorry, I don't know why it's making me so emotional."

I looked at Angellica and then back to Kelly. I just blurt out my first thought, "Kels, are you pregnant?"

"Huh? What? Why would you think that?" She gets up to start gathering stuff for breakfast. She's avoiding my gaze, but I stand at the island, observing.

"Context clues. Getting overly emotional over something so simple, bringing up your hormones, and I know I was drunk yesterday, and so was Angellica when she danced around with a lampshade on her head, but you maintained a clear head. I can bet there was no liquor in your cup! You're pregnant!" I was jumping and squealing loudly, which did not help my hangover, but it was worth it.

"Alright, alright, alright! I found out a few days ago and was going to tell him at the holiday party, but I'm so scared of how he might react. I know this might be asking too much from you, but will you come with me tonight so I can tell him? I need the support."

Coming face to face with Santa so soon? Kelly was growing to be like a sister, and I wanted to be a part of her exciting news.

"Sure. What's the dress code?"

"Uh, cocktail casual."

"What does that even mean?!"

"Just wear a sexy dress. Do you want to punish him a bit? Be a bombshell but flirt a little. If he wants you, he'll claim you. I know Nick; he doesn't want to get hurt again. Angellica, you come, too! A sweet girl needs to gain some suitors. We'll all come over here to get ready. The party starts at 8 p.m. tonight, but we can be fashionably late."

"What if I get too much attention? You know... I only want to be there to support you."

"Then we'll leave, simple as that. Although I'm mad, I should make the big lug lunch. See you gals later."

"Okay, bye, moooooom." She cut her eyes and then laughed, rubbing her nonexistent stomach. I'm so happy for her.

Angel and I both get dressed and head to the shop. There are still a few admirers. I signed a few autographs and turned down a couple of guys. The gleam in their eyes was so offputting. Each chime of the bell had my heart racing, thinking it would be Nick, but every time, I was disappointed. This time was no different, but at least it was a friendly face.

"Hey, Xav."

"Beautiful. How are you?"

"Not enjoying my newfound fame, but what can I do?"

He holds up a white paper bag. "I brought you lunch. Come spend 15 minutes with me."

I could smell something delicious wafting from the bag and was curious. I looked back to see Angel; her expressionless face said it all. He seems harmless, so I follow him outside to the closest bench by the door. He opens the bag, pulls out a slice of pepperoni pizza, and hands it to me. He also has parmesan and red pepper. I placed it on my lap and opened it, inhaling the deliciousness.

"It smells amazing, but didn't you get a slice for yourself?" He slides closer, "There's enough to share. Why don't you feed me a bite? Add that cheese and pepper, too."

I added the whole packet of red pepper and a bit of cheese. I was not blind to the fact that he was intimately close to me and now he wanted me to feed him. I tear off a piece and he leans in even further as I pop it in his mouth.

"Mmm, so delicious, especially coming from those finger-tips." I dig in and am delightfully in bliss over this delicious pizza.

"Yum, where is this from?"

"Peter's pizzeria, which is over there in the back corner. It's the town's best-kept secret. I thought you would love it...and I'd earn some bonus points."

He smiles wide as I break off another piece for myself and one for him, but he holds his hand up. "I brought it for you. I'll grab something on the way back to the cafe.

His arm was on top of the bench as he faced me. He had sat back, but he was still in my personal space.

"So, do you have any plans this evening?" He grabbed a napkin, wiping sauce away from the corner of my mouth.

"I'm going with Kelly to the holiday party at the fire station."

"Oh, is that tonight? Sounds utterly boring. If you get tired, maybe you can stop by my place afterward?" He paused while waiting for me to respond, but I took a big bite to avoid any decision-making. "Ok, let me propose somewhere more neutral but fun. How about the town holiday festival tomorrow? We can have hot cocoa, enjoy the cringey music, and perhaps take a lap on the ice rink. It'll put you back in the holiday spirit. I want your first town Christmas celebration in Asher Falls to be memorable."

Boy has it.

He leans in closer, "You have options, Elivia. Much better options are right in front of you. Give me a chance. Just smile and nod." He smiled as he stretched out his hand and grabbed my chin, moving it up and down. "Sure thing, Xavier. I'd love to hang out with you. You are such a stud muffin, the hottest guy in town." He said in a terrible falsetto of what was supposed to be my voice. Then his hand opened up, and he placed it on my cheek. Then there was silence. He was closing the gap between us...

"Hey Livi, do we need to order more...oh! Sor-sorry!" Angellica about-faced so fast; seeing how super close we were to each other made me scoot away to gather my thoughts.

He sighed and reached for my hand, squeezing it lightly and kissing my cheek. "Just a friend...taking out a friend." He sounded so convincing; what was the harm if he put it that way? I agreed. "Okay, but this is not a date!"

"Whatever you say. If you happen to slip and I catch you, what's a kiss between friends?" With that, he gets up and heads towards his car.

"Eww. I don't trust him." Angellica says sternly, leaning against the door as I come in.

"Why not? It's a friendly outing."

"Come on, Livi, it's a date! Everyone knows Xavier has had eyes on you. He moves in silence, but he's overly charming, sugary sweet to get what he wants, and he wants you in his bed!"

"No, he's one of those suave and flirtatious types. I'm

allowed to hang out with guys. Besides, it's not like I was in a relationship with Nick. We just slept together. I was something he could brag about. That's it."

She looked me up and down, "Keep telling yourself that and eventually you'll start to believe it, but I don't. I'm going to grab my stuff and then I'll be at your place." She shook her head before grabbing her keys. I stood there replaying what she was saying. Was I kidding myself?

Once I got home, I took a shower. I was conflicted about what to wear, especially since everyone knew I was a lingerie model. They've all basically seen me at least half-naked, if not more. I stood in my closet, looking at all my options.

"You should wear the sexiest dress to make heads turn and jaws drop. You won't have that body forever. Soon, you'll be a whale like me."

"Kels, you're not even showing yet."

"Yeah, well, I feel like one. I'm tired and bloated. I threw up three times today! This kid is already wreaking havoc, but Mama will wow everyone in this dress. Listen, whatever you pick is going to be perfect. The more important decision is if you want to throw what you have away. To answer, who do you really want to be with? Nick or Xavier?"

"Xavier is just a friend."

"HA! Don't be naive! He wants his shot, and apparently, he's been doubling down since the big reveal. Angel told me about what happened earlier. It's a slippery slope, girl." She tuts, then puts her hand on her stomach, "Oh, Mama has to pee again. Ugh, it's always something with him."

"How do you know it's a boy this early?"

"Only men cause this much trouble." I couldn't help but burst out laughing. After settling down, I chose a red ruched party dress with black heels. I would wear my off-white pea coat to battle the chilly weather. I defined my waves and did a bold lip and a more neutral eye. Ruby red lips were a must-have during the holidays.

After putting it all together, I helped Angellica pick her makeup look. We went with a smokey green eye and a more neutral nude lip. She did finger waves and wore a simple little black dress. She looked like a flapper girl from the 20s without the jewelry. Kelly walks out in a 60s-style red dress that has a petticoat underneath. She looked like the women in Good Housekeeping magazine smiling while holding up their award-winning pie.

"We look like we belong in three different eras."

"But we all look amazing. Livi, that dress is hot! He won't be able to keep his eyes off you."

"That's not the point." I reiterate. They look at each other and laugh, grabbing their coats, and we're off to see Santa and his elves.

19

NICK

I'd rather be sulking at home, but I have a job to do. I shake my feet and those annoying little bells jingle. I look like a Christmas-themed fool. My new role was to help guide the children to Santa when it was their turn to take a picture with him. Beck was doing a great job as Santa. He was jovial and upbeat, ensuring each one left with a big smile. Those kids would have seen right through me. I still try to portray the happy elf coming down from Santa's village, taking a break from making toys to make sure they each get their time with Santa. Every kid smiled and thanked me when I handed them a gift bag filled with candy, toys, and trinkets.

"HO HO HO, and welcome to Santa's village hosted by the Asher Falls fire department! Don't forget to pick up a special treat from one of my merry elves!"

A little boy tugged on my sleeve, and I perched down to his level; he couldn't be older than five. "You're my favorite elf." And he hugged me, waving when his mother walked him towards our spread of food. The way his face lit up warmed my heart. I started wondering what kind of parent I would be.

"Alright, kiddies, Santa's going to take a small break! Be back in ten minutes. We have plenty of games for you to play."

I follow him to the back, where he snatches off the hat and beard in the upstairs dorm where the kids can't see.

"I'm exhausted! Little terrors they are. Okay, not all of them. Did you see Kendra brought her snot-nosed hellions?"

"Yeah. She tried to cop a feel, openly grabbing for my dick. She's like, 'Damn Nick, you still look good. What do you say I meet you for a nightcap after I put the kids to bed?' Blecch! I guess she forgot about how she got pregnant with her youngest, Cody, while we were together. And isn't she still with that guy, what's his name?"

Beck shrugs, "I think they are married."

I stood at the railing, looking down at the festivities. "That's even worse. Forget her, I couldn't care less because I can't stop thinking about..." I stopped because the object of my desire was here. She, Kelly, and I think her name is Angellica checked their coats in, and she looked phenomenal. It's a simple yet sexy little red number.

"Elivia. She looks stunning. I can't believe you convinced Kelly to ask her to come."

"I didn't. Kelly said she asked her here for support, whatever that meant. Meanwhile, I'm going to apologize to my wife. You should at least say hello."

I looked down, regretting my decision to swap my role. "Like this?!" He chuckles, then tries to stop before it gets out of control, "Humble yourself for the girl you claim you want. Or you may miss your only chance."

He was right. I pulled up my tights and went back downstairs. She was looking around. I was hoping she was looking for me. I snuck around until I was behind her. She's used to sexy Santa and not this stupid elf version of me.

"Hey." She jumped and screeched a bit. I thought she'd still be mad, but she's laughing hysterically.

"Okay, it's not that funny."

"I'm sorry, I'm sorry!! But why aren't you playing Santa?"

"I gave it up because of my mood; I would have been a crap Santa. My heart wasn't in it. Now I'm Jingles McSnowflake, head of the gift shop elves."

"Jingles Mcwhat?! Oh my gosh, it just keeps getting better!" She wipes the tears from her eyes. It's good to see her smile, even at my expense. Then, the awkward silence settled in. I rub my neck, trying not to stare at her beautiful form.

"You look breathtaking."

She pulled her hair behind her ear while looking down. "Thank you."

"Elivia." I hear someone call her, but I'm distracted when I see a hand wrap around her waist.

She looks just as surprised as I am, "Xavier, what are you doing here?"

Because there was no reason for him to be here but to try and establish his dominance, that motherfucker just stepped into my territory.

I'm trying not to react openly, like slamming his face onto the concrete floor.

"Well, *mi amor*, I couldn't wait until our festival rendezvous tomorrow to see you; plus, I knew you'd be wearing something absolutely stunning, and I was right." He takes her hands, steps back to look at her, and then turns my way.

"Nick, you look..." He looks away to laugh, but he doesn't cover it up. He's feeding off of it.

My hatred for the guy who had to lie to look good in her eyes is multiplying astronomically. I sincerely hoped she wasn't buying into this bullshit.

"You look like a clown, a Christmas freak!" He blurts out loudly while putting his hands in his pockets.

Before I could explode, she turned toward him, "He's in costume to entertain the children! You're really pathetic picking on someone who obviously cares about his community. What are you doing to make a difference?"

He looked as surprised as I was; by now, there was a bit of attention on us.

"Are you saying you'd pick him over me? Look at me; I'm the hottest thing in town, sweetie. You and I make sense. A hot guy and a supermodel..."

"I am not a damn supermodel! I don't want that to be my entire life! It's vain and pretentious and just not me! It's like," She sighs and pinches the bridge of her nose. "Get out..."

She said it calmly and walked toward the back of the fire-house. He stood there before walking behind her, but I cut him off. Beck and a few others surround us. He was close enough for me to take out my rage and frustration, but I was not going to ruin this event for the kids.

I step close to him, talking through my gritted teeth, "Get the fuck out before I rearrange your face for the lies you told."

"You think she'd picked a pathetic excuse of a man over me? You're not even in her league. It was a pity fuck...mama's boy. I'll get the job done right." Then he smirked.

I saw a white-hot flash streak behind my eyes before I saw Beck jump in front of the punch I was about to throw. He grabs Xav by his arm, "You're done, get out!" Beck shoves him back-ward and Jackson pushes him out the side door to cause less commotion.

I needed to release this anger, but with so many people, all I could do was go back and slam my fist against my locker. These were no cheap school-grade aluminum lockers; it was real solid metal, and the pain took my mind off causing pain. I shake my hand, which causes a stinging as my joints pop with the flicking.

"Ugh, I should have ended him on sight. Screw rules and decency!"

"You think that would have been a good idea? At your job? What if she saw that? Trust me, you did the right thing."

I cut my eyes at Beck, and he held up his hands, allowing me to take a deep breath and calm down. Then he starts to chuckle, which turns into a laugh, which causes me to laugh.

"Dude, you were ready to end him!"

"Still am. I'm trying to calm down before..."

"Nick?" There was Elivia at the top of the stairs. She noticed I was clenching my hand. "Are you hurt?!" She walks up and grabs my hands. It hurts, but I try not to flinch because even this small gesture of her touching me is special.

"No, I'm fine."

"You are not fine. I'm sorry, what he said was so fucking rude." She didn't hear what else he spat after she left.

"He's not worth even talking about." I can see Beck backing down the stairs with a smile on his face as he clips on his Santa beard. She looks behind her and then sits down on a bunk, my bunk, actually. To know there's a chance I could smell her perfume while I'm on shift excites me. She pats the bed next to me, "I'm sorry, Nick. You shouldn't have been ridiculed like that. What you do for this community is amazing. All your volunteer work and your job? You are a hero. I wish he never showed up here to rile you up." She huffed in disgust. It was good to know she could see through his bullshit.

I chuckled while rubbing my hands together, "You can make it up to me..."

"Meaning?"

"How about Santa escorting Mrs. Claus to the town festival? Can we start over?" I hold out my hand and she takes it. It's a long silence between us, but it isn't awkward.

"Okay."

I can hear Beck call for everyone's attention and we both head down the stairs back to the party. We caught him at the beginning of his speech. Livi stands beside Kelly and me next to my best friend.

"My beautiful wife, who I fall in love with more and more each day; this gift symbolizes all the time we've been together and how much you mean to me. I don't want to fight. I want to lay in bed with you and fall asleep, whispering how much I love you. No gift could explain how much I love you, but this is my sad attempt."

He hands her a card and Tiffany's bag. She has him hold the bag as she retrieves the box. She opens it up to see a pair of emerald earrings and a matching necklace. "Oh my gosh! Tyler, it's the set I always wanted! They are beautiful!" She pulls off the necklace she wore to put it on. She wrapped her arms around him, and he squeezed her tightly, but she backed away quickly, placing her hand over her mouth. She holds her other hand up as Elivia steps forward. "Are you gonna be sick?" Kelly adamantly shook her head, no, but said she needed a few moments.

Beck looks very concerned. "Honey, do we need to go to the hospital? Nick can take over as Santa. We can go right now." Now, he sounded frantic, but she placed her hands on his chest, and he seemed to calm down visibly. She asked Angellica for the bag she was holding.

"I'm fine. Here, I brought my most important gift to you. Open it." He didn't seem convinced she was alright but reached into the bag anyway and pulled out a flat box. He opens it and promptly shuts it, "Shut up!" Kelly starts crying, and Elivia is wiping away a stray tear.

"Beck, what is it?!" I ask. His smile is so wide as he reveals a onesie that says *Baby Beckham due soon* and three positive pregnancy tests.

He picks her up and spins her. "We're having a baby? We're having a baby!" The whole firehouse erupts in applause and whistles.

"Beck, please! My nausea." She looked even paler than the first incident. He walked away and came back, "Ginger ale, babydoll. You've made this the best Christmas ever."

She smiles, "It is. I do have one thing to ask someone." Then she turns to Elivia. "You've been an amazing friend and you're the only one I would trust to be my baby's godmother." She gasped and stared at Kelly in complete shock.

"Me? Really?! I-I, of course!"

Kelly made a great decision. She'll love that baby with all her heart. "I'm so honored to be a godmother! Thank you, both of you. I won't let you down!" She hugs both of them, raising the hem of her dress a bit and I remember when those soft legs were once wrapped around me. Only I would turn a touching moment into something so tawdry.

"And Nick, you should know I want you as the godfather. Uncle Nick has such a nice ring to it." She locks eyes with me, and I clear my throat, looking at Beck. "Of course, I'd be honored." He claps my back and then quickly gives Kelly a kiss. "You're the best thing to happen to me, babe. I have to get back to Santa-ing, but I love you!"

I'm awkwardly standing with the girls, "Uhh, I should also get back to my elfly duties. I'll see you at the festival?" She nods as I head back to my duties as Santa's head elf.

Tomorrow, I need to show that I saw her heart before I knew her past and one day, I hope she's comfortable talking to me about her old life. We both share a type of pain, mine with my parent's death and her traumatized by extreme beauty standards and superficial men. She was classically beautiful to me, but it simply wasn't enough in that world. I wanted to be a comforting ear. I had to do this right and give her that cheesy romantic movie moment she's been waiting for. She was worth it.

Elivia

NICK WALKED AWAY and I felt sad knowing I was going home alone. His attitude seemed to improve as he interacted with the kids. He looks horrendous in his costume but doesn't seem to mind as much now. Making those kids smile seemed to be his priority.

He's going to make a great godfather.

As the kids started to head home, all the holiday characters disappeared. Returning in their normal clothes to indulge in the alcohol.

"Elivia." I turned to see Beckham. "Can we chat?" I nod and he escorts me to a quiet corner of the firehouse. "Let me start by apologizing; my wording was chauvinistic and barbaric. I was thrilled to see Nick finally excited about someone. He's never been this hopeful before, but I promise you, he was not bragging in a cocky sense. He wanted to share his feelings of happiness about you. That's all." He held up his hand like a boy scout. I could tell he was sincere.

"I believe you and this might be a big misunderstanding, but I need time. Do you know that the day after I confronted him, I holed up and broke down in my office after being bombarded by so-called fans? By the way, a few of your buddies were there. It's exhausting. I just want to be me and to have a quiet life. I do appreciate your words, though."

"You make him happy; I'll leave you with that. On another note, I am thankful for you being the friend that Kelly needs. Enjoy the rest of your night."

"You, too." He hugged me and I was not ready for that. He holds his hand out and Kelly takes it as they head home to celebrate their growing family.

"Hey." I don't even need to look. I know it's Nick. He has my coat in his hands. "May I?" I agree and he slips it over my shoulder.

"So...I'll meet you at the festival after my shift?"

"I would like that."

"I want to spend time with you and see that smile. And also, I want to see you watching me win the competition. Good luck, though. You had an amazing display... for a newbie." Then he smiled, the one that gave me butterflies.

I rolled my eyes but laughed at that jab, "Thanks, but I, uhh, dropped out of the competition after our last night, and I cast my vote for you. No one could beat such a beautiful and heart-warming display, Nick. I really hope you win. Have a good night." I turn to make my way to my car.

"You, too." He almost whispered.

I got home and retired to my room for a hot shower. My mind was all over the place. I wanted more than anything for Nick to sweep me off my feet, but he was treading lightly after I blew up at him. I leaned against my window and saw that his light was on, but it turned off. I didn't know if he was still there peeking through the break in the curtains, but I admit part of me was hoping he was as I let the robe slip off my shoulders before I climbed into bed, my head and heart heavy. I know it wasn't malicious. He's been so good to me. I was going to fix it tomorrow and start fresh with Nick.

The last-minute buyers were rampant the next morning and I made sure they felt guilty about buying on Christmas Eve. Most of them went above their budget because their women deserved it. I was playing two characters, Cupid, by helping them, but also the ghost of Christmas Future, showing them if they're not thoughtful next time, they'll wind up in big trouble.

I went home for lunch and ate quickly while walking around the house to stay awake. I would have to go to the festival straight from work. I changed into a white sweater dress and paired it with my red peacoat and beret. I wore flat black riding boots for comfort. It was a modern take on Mrs. Claus.

It was almost closing time at the store when I was startled by the sirens and lights of the fire engine as it raced toward the downtown area. It was going so fast I couldn't see who was on board. I watched until it disappeared, but I could still faintly hear it. It changed the tone of the atmosphere. I tried to focus on the beauty of the decorations that led up to the staging area. The streets were beautifully adorned with huge white light snowflakes at the top of the streetlights and Christmas gift boxes around the base with white string lights wrapped around with a string crossing above the road to the other side, obviously high enough for the fire truck to get by. Storefronts displayed their holiday best, and you could see everything from gingerbread towns to train sets, Santa's village, of course, and a daycare where the kids made Santa faces with cotton balls.

If I had kids, I'd love to see their artwork displayed like this.

What a wayward thought.

The townspeople were walking to the stage area in front of a red and white striped tent. A table on the stage was filled with ribbons and trophies. The grand prize was substantially larger than the other and came with one of those giant obnoxious ribbon buttons like you see at livestock shows.

It was still early as the vendors continued to set up their booths. There was an arts and crafts pavilion where I needed to shop to buy something unique for my mom and friends back in New York. Next to those vendors were the food stands with kettle corn, cinnamon sugar roasted almonds, hot cocoa, and soft gingerbread men. The next set of vendors had trailers instead of tents. Those held the more substantial foods, such as chimney cakes and waffles. Also, there was a beverage truck with hot chocolate, mulled wine, kinder punch, and wassail. And for those with a voracious appetite, in the back corner was a smoker/cooker filled with delicious meats, from turkey legs to ham, sausages, and skewers. My stomach growled as I perused all my options. I grabbed a quick skewer to tide myself over as I walked around.

The ice rink was up and running. The air was filled with laughter, screaming, and gleeful shouting from the kids with the skate trainers, to teenagers obviously on a date but disguising it as a 'group outing' and my favorite, the dad with his three daughters. They skate better than Daddy, but he doesn't mind falling to hear their laughs and see their smiles; it's so wholesome.

Now that I think about it, I haven't skated since college. Once I started modeling, anything that could cause bodily harm was detrimental to my career. That meant no bumps, bruises, marks, or scrapes. I was actually looking forward to getting out there and ending up on my ass, laughing hysterically. Nick would help me up and make sure I was okay before he grabbed my hand and we circled around, enjoying each other's company.

Sigh.

I knew it wouldn't happen because he was responding to whatever emergency was happening right now. My ears still picked up on the fire truck sirens in the distance. It gave me an uneasy feeling in my stomach.

"Elivia." I turn to see Xavier headed my way. I forgot I agreed to meet him here. Shit!

"I'm glad to see you. Now I can show you I'm a better choice than some crybaby mama's boy."

Now I saw the pompous, egotistical bullshit that I saw in New York. He was being overly sweet, but underneath that shell was an asshole. I turned to walk away, but he grabbed my arm. I snatched away quickly, "Don't fucking touch me. Everybody was trying to warn me. Livi, he just wants to bag you; he's trying too hard; he wants you in his bed, and judging by your behavior yesterday, I believe them. Look me in the eye and tell me that's not true."

He looked shocked and hurt that I would accuse him of such a thing, but then this slimy smile appeared. "The opportunity to bang a supermodel? Who the hell wouldn't try?! It's bragging rights. So, let's ditch this stupid celebration and warm up at my place. I'll make sure you realize I'm a much better fuck than Nick."

"Is that all you want?" He shrugs and I am disgusted. "Glad to know that." He smiled, thinking I was applauding him for his honesty, and as he got close enough, I kneed him. He crumpled like a sack of potatoes; he couldn't scream out in pain.

"Ohhhh...sorry. Guess you won't be able to perform now, tonight, or probably the next few weeks." I kneeled down to his fallen frame. People looked but kept on their merry way. "I would choose Nick over you any day because the sparks are there, the feelings are there, and he's sincere about how he feels for me. If you want to fuck someone famous, go to New York. Stay far away from me, you pompous troll."

He couldn't even reply over his labored and painful breathing. I stroll away with a smile on my face. Nick would be proud.

Attention! We will be announcing the winners of the contest in ten minutes.

Saved by the announcement. Even though I was no longer in the running, I was curious to see if Nick would get his Cinderella story and win for his parents. I make my way toward the stage.

They were announcing the winners for the businesses. The cute little daycare center took first place, but who would be surprised? Adorable children's drawings always win our hearts. Next are the apartments/condos, then townhomes, then houses. I scream loudly when Angellica wins second place for her decorations. She looked so proud as she grinned while holding her trophy and ribbon.

As I was going toward the stage to congratulate her, there was a large boom and a huge flash of light coming from the direction of the fire. Then a plume of smoke. A nearby officer's radio cracked and hissed before he turned the knob up as high as it would go:

All emergency services in Harris and nearby counties respond immediately to the Pike granary and farm northwest of Asher Falls. Five-alarm fire with casualties, I repeat, we have casualties. Respond immediately!

Nick!

20

NICK

It was Christmas Eve and the day of the town's celebration and awards ceremony. I wanted to win the competition and celebrate with her. I was still taken aback that she dropped out and voted for me to win. It was a selfless gesture.

I had a whole plan to romance her. If I couldn't finish it today, I would do it on Christmas Day. Last night, after she got home and stared in my window for a while before going to bed, I found myself in an emotional rabbit hole watching the Hallmark channel with those super cheesy holiday movies...for research.

In the second movie, the man tells the woman to meet him at this gazebo in the middle of town to explain. She's hesitant, fighting her emotions, but ends up there just as a light flurry starts. He pours his heart out, and you can see the moment her heart bursts, he pulls her in for a long kiss, then he lifts her up and gives her the kiss like Elivia described while sitting on my lap at the shopping center. Then the sappy music played with the snow increasing and it was happily ever after. I can see the appeal and wanted to be exactly what she needed. I wanted her to feel comfortable coming to my place as I am to hers. Truth be told, I prefer the coziness of her place. Her place was perfect for a couple and my place was good for when the couple expanded their family.

I couldn't stop thinking about the possibilities. Nothing was going to stop me from...

Beep beep beep beep

"Every. Single. Time! ARGH!" I threw on my T-shirt and raced out the door to the firehouse. I parked haphazardly and sprinted in to start throwing on my gear. "Where's the call?!" I yell.

"Suspicious activity at the old granary!"

Suspicious indeed because it hadn't been functional in at least eight years. Maybe the Pikes were resuming business or selling the land to someone. I guess we will find out.

Since the fire was categorized as a three-alarm already, the whole company would respond, so we took both trucks. I had to hyperfocus to slide onto the aerial with my gear. It's a dangerous game being distracted.

"Move your ass, St. Nick!" My best friend screams from the truck.

I was able to get on after throwing my stuff up first. "Thanks for your words of encouragement, Beck." Not mentioning that hearing St. Nick riles my fantasies about her screaming it at the top of her lungs in climax.

"I do what I can." We suddenly take a sharp left and Jackson yells back, "Sorry! Detour because of the festival! Taking the rural road!"

Obviously, the back road isn't as maintained, so it was a bit...bumpy. When he took another sharp turn, I slammed my back against the inside of the cab.

"Take it easy, Jackson! I'll need medical attention before we reach the fire!"

"Sorry! Old man Richards' sheep were about to cross the road. I mean, I love a good lamb chop and all..."

"Wow, brutal." Beck laughs while tightening up his jacket.

We could see the smoke better as we approached but were still unsure of the source.

"50 bucks says it's the silo. Probably a fully functioning meth lab they tried to cover up."

"Damn, Perry, really? I think it's a controlled burn that got out of hand. Remember, Pike Farm used to have the best produce in the county before the owner died and his kids abandoned the place. Maybe someone came back to revive it. What's your guess, Nicholas?"

I hadn't even thought about it. I could see the smoke was thick and black. From what I can see, I assumed, "Equipment fire. Probably tried to crank up that old tractor entwined in those thick bushes."

"We'll find out in two minutes. Equipment check!"

I check Beck's tank meters and vice versa when we stop.

It was worse than any guess; the barn and the silo were ablaze, lighting up the twilight sky but also billowing a cloud of thick, noxious smoke. Not only that but there were secondary fires from the mini explosions from whatever was housed in either building.

"We're first, but more are coming from the surrounding counties. Start from the fields and work your way toward the main fire. Nicolas on the hose! Everyone be vigilant. The condition of the structure is still unknown."

I quickly lift the cabin high; even at max height, the fire towers even higher, and the heat is intense. I wait for my cue as I watch Beck, Perry, and Jackson turn the hose on to combat the brush fire as they walk slowly toward the building. For normal people, the first instinct says to spray immediately, but that could cause problems, including increased smoke that reduces visibility; the pressure of the water can compromise the integrity of the structure and could create a collapse, or I could simply run out of water, so timing is critical.

"Nick, get ready. Once we go in and gauge structural integrity, we can cover the inside while you saturate the top." Beck radioed as they got even closer to the door. He started coughing and signaled for everyone to don their masks.

"Be careful, Beck. We don't know what materials are inside!" I shouted before I had to put on my mask after they hit it with the first wave of water and the smoke increased exponentially.

"Roger that."

While waiting, I looked over and saw the string lights where the celebration was held. I knew that she was there. Although I'm not there to show her around, I hope she's enjoying the festivities. I can surprise her if we get this under control with the other engine companies.

I looked down to see them positioned at the door. Jackson had an axe in hand if they couldn't get in manually.

"Nicholas, open hose!" The radio crackled. I opened full blast aiming at a hole in the silo, not the barn they were walking into.

"No origin yet. Nick, do y... see ...ames... there?" I was able to figure out what he was asking through the breaks. I look around and radio back.

"Origin is in the rear of the barn connected to the silo. Secondary fire involves the old tractor." As I suspected. I didn't expect us all to be right; it was all on fire.

I knew he was going to tell me to spray the primary and get that controlled, so I moved my spray to the junction of the buildings. The heat coming off of it was almost unbearable in all this gear and the smoke was only getting thicker. I could barely see the ground below but hear them through the comms.

"Beck report in!"

"There's ...something blocking the door to ... silo. Can't get in that way! Going to reverse and go around from the outside... Keep spraying!"

"Alright." I lowered the boom to concentrate the stream into the opening. I looked around to see if there were any companies within view. I saw some lights coming over a hill from the west, undoubtedly Hermann company. They were about 15 miles from Asher Falls. I sighed in relief to be getting some help and for them getting out of the building; it wasn't a stable structure to begin with. I saw three bodies walking backward out the door.

I felt a moment of happiness. It was short-lived, though, as part of the roof collapsed, nearly catching them and causing a slow-motion reaction. The debris added kindling to the fire, which caused a white-hot flash explosion. I heard them scream before the comms went out. I looked down and they were scattered on the ground. I started lowering the boom when a secondary but stronger explosion happened, and I knew it was stronger because it caused the truck to teeter.

It was at that moment I realized...

We hadn't anchored the truck.

I was frozen in fear. There was nothing I could do...

The truck was blown backward.

I was freefalling in the cabin...

21

ELIVIA

The entire crowd gasped. There were a couple of shrieks and screams, and some kids started to cry.

"Nick!" I screamed, then clamped my hands over my mouth. I looked around frantically. I don't know what for, but I was relieved to see Kelly in the crowd, and she heard me scream.

"Livi!" She came over and hugged me. Kelly and I looked back to the West; the fire was now visible from where we were. I immediately became nauseous.

"What do we do?! Do we go there? I have my car; let's go!" I sounded like a mad woman. Kelly grabbed my hands, "Stop. Whatever happened has happened and there's nothing we can do but wait at the hospital. Whether they are hurt or not, they have to get medically cleared by the doctor. Come on, I'll drive."

"But you're pregnant."

"And you're freaking out. You're not thinking straight, and I'm fine. I'm not new to this; besides, they have to check everyone for smoke inhalation; it's pretty routine, especially for fires above two alarms."

She's right. I can't even explain what I'm feeling or hearing in my thoughts. I'm almost in tears and there's a lump in my throat.

"Come on, the hospital is down the road. You'll meet some of the other girlfriends and wives. They can give you advice, especially being a newbie."

"But I'm not..."

She smiles while starting the engine, signaling to exit the parking lot. "Sweetie, how you reacted shows love and concern. You care for him and that's okay. You're allowed to worry about Nick. If roles were reversed, he'd tear down a building with a single axe until he knew you were safe."

I felt a little warmth, knowing he would make sure I was okay, and I was going to do the same for him.

At the hospital, Kelly seemed to know where to go as we approached a group of women in the waiting room.

"Kelly! We thought you hadn't heard. We were going to send Mindy to your house. Have you heard anything?" A worried-looking redhead said as she hugged Kelly. Her green eyes filled to the brim with tears and worry.

"Not yet. I wanted to introduce Elivia to our group."

She looked over at me, tightening her sweater. "Oh, nice to meet you. Wait, you're that model girl everyone was talking about!" I cringe, thinking she might chastise me for her husband ogling me or something about the state of my moral compass. I mean, I couldn't blame her if she did. I shrugged, bracing for it, "Yeah."

She touches my shoulder, "Don't worry; there is no judgment here. Besides, I'd love to hear some exciting big-city stories while we wait for them to come in. Get my mind off the negative thoughts."

She pats my hand, and we laugh, "I'll answer whatever you want. Anything to take my mind off of...this." I waved my hand around. Here I was, waiting in an emergency room to find out the status of the man I cut off a couple of days ago. We were going to start over. I felt my throat tighten and I think she noticed.

"Oh, sweetie, we're all here as support. Come on." We walk over to the women sitting in a circle. You could see the worry on their faces even though they were trying to maintain positivity.

Kelly sat down, "Everyone, this is Elivia."

A blonde lady studied me and then pointed, "I think it's finally happened, ladies!" They all chuckle and I felt out of the loop. Kelly nods her head, "You are right. Our resident sweetheart, Nick, finally met his match. Livi, this is Piper, Jas, Hime, Mindy, and Taye."

"Ni-nice to meet you, ladies." Piper, the redhead, hands me a hot cocoa. "Here, it calms the nerves. If you need it, we got shots of whiskey." She reaches into her bag to pull out two mini bottles. A few of the ladies indicate that's what might be in their cup.

"No, this is enough, thank you." I sip and sigh loudly, "How do you not freak out? He and I aren't even official yet. In fact, I kind of broke off whatever this was, but we were reconciling, yet my stomach and heart dropped when they said there were casualties. What if he's...?" I place my hand on my heart to calm the beating in my chest after even uttering those dreadful words.

Kelly squeezed my hand, "We don't think that way. Our guys are strong and experienced. They'll be okay, alright? That's what you get for being the new blood." They all chuckle, seeing this is not their first rodeo for some. Kelly claps her hands, then points, "Do you guys remember the Winnie wildfire? It was my first incident with Beck. I worked myself up so much I passed out, and when I came to, I was looking at a very angry husband, but then he was relieved to see I was okay." They all nod in agreement.

Then she stretched and rubbed her stomach.

"Are you hungry? Do you want me to go to the cafeteria and

grab you something?" As the godmother, I felt I was responsible for keeping her nourished until we found out if Beck was okay.

"I wish we were still at the festival; I could get some slices of ham and... cotton candy. Doesn't that sound yummy? The combination of sweet and salty? Like a taco."

I tried not to gag openly; whether or not I was turning green physically was another story.

Kelly huffed, "Whatever, Livi! Wait until you're carrying Nick's baby; the cravings won't make sense to nobody but you."

I stood there with my mouth open because it was like a shot to the gut, knocking the wind out of me.

Everyone heard her and I had no response.

"I...uhh..."

Then the emergency doors burst open, and three firefighters walked in on their own accord, holding their equipment. The nurses guided them to one of the empty bays as they coughed and wheezed. They were covered in soot but no worse for the wear. The spouses follow behind their men. I squeeze Kelly's hand a bit tighter as I hear the sirens of an ambulance. The doors open with a gurney, "I've got head trauma and a possible broken arm!" The EMT yells.

"Take him to trauma two!" A nurse says, guiding them to the appropriate room. One glance and I recognized Beck. Kelly gasped, "Tyler!" His head moved side to side as he fought to catch his breath. "Kel-ly..." He said weakly as he held his hand up. He was bleeding through the makeshift bandage. Her hands instantly connected with his as they made their way to the back.

Then another set of guys walked in, but none were Nick. Some of them had different uniforms; perhaps they were from surrounding area departments. I was a standing army of one and felt utter dread. I hugged myself to feel comfortable, but it didn't work. I let my head fall along with my tears until a pair of boots were in my view. I gasped but frowned when I saw Bryson's massive frame.

He hugged Taye, who I assumed was his wife, and then they looked at me. "Just tell me! Is he..." I cried as Taye held me up against her.

"Hey, hey, hey. No, he's not dead. There was an explosion that knocked us all on our ass, but then there was a second and stronger explosion that knocked the fire truck off balance, and...well, Nick was in the cherry picker, and it fell backward."

"What?!" That's all I could say from the shock and my creativity is concocting all these terrible fatal scenarios. My imagination was working against me.

"He's alive but unconscious. He should be coming in momentarily; the ambulance pulled up behind us."

Right on cue, the doors swing open again, "Get him to ICU stat! We need to locate the bleeding before he hemorrhages!"

Those were not the words I needed to hear. I saw his sweat-drenched and soot-ridden face, but he wasn't moving. "Nick!" I screamed.

ICU, uncontrollable bleeding, hemorrhaging...critical.

The room is spinning and it's more than I can bear.

I don't know how long I had been out, but I was now lying in a hospital bed. I sat up fast. "Hey, no, you need to calm down. You already fainted once." Kelly gave me that mom look but also a look of concern.

"Oh, my head. How long was I out?"

"Almost four hours. You were also dehydrated, so they gave you fluids. You needed to rest, but you kept calling for Nick. I'm sorry I wasn't there when I was tending to Beck. I should have been there." She chastised herself, but I shook my head, "Absolutely not, he's your husband, and he was hurt. I expected that. Seeing Nick like that was too much, especially with so much unknown. Are there any updates?"

I didn't notice another person until Beck pushed himself off the wall with his good shoulder, his other in a sling, and a bandage around his arm and head.

"Hey, Beck, I'm glad you're okay."

He gave me his best side hug. It wasn't awkward like before; it was brotherly with a kiss on my forehead, "Hey, kiddo. Glad you're awake. Nick was in the picker, and it was a 30-foot fall. They're checking for broken bones and head trauma; supposedly, there might be internal bleeding, but they'll find that, too. He's been in surgery for a couple of hours now. I'm his next of kin, so I'll get updates."

It all sounded serious, maybe even fatal. I started to cry again, "I didn't fix it. I should have fixed us! What if it's too late? I never got to say that I'm sorry." I wallow in my tears and bury my head in my hands.

"Listen, we'll be right back."

I closed my eyes, hoping it would all be a bad dream. A few minutes later, Kelly returns, "Beck's getting an update, and you are cleared to go home. We'll drop you off, then Tyler and I will grab some clothes. I'm staying with you and he's staying at Nick's. Angellica's coming over, too."

"I'm not the best company right now. Technically, it's Christmas. You two should be together, opening gifts and doing cute Christmas couple stuff."

She pulls the chair up to my bed and takes my hands, "Nick would kill me if I didn't take care of you, including spending Christmas together. We don't mind; we're practically family. I know he's worried about you, even if he is unconscious. Face it, Livi, you're it for him. Whatever problem you two had means nothing. When he wakes up, and he will, mark it as day one of your lives together. Now, the nurse should have your discharge paperwork soon. We'll eat a quick bite, and you will get some rest. No arguments! Then we'll have a traditional dinner later tonight."

I hold my hands up, "You got the mom tone down already. I

won't put up a fight." It was another 45 minutes before I was released. I desperately wanted to see him, but he was still in surgery.

Beck spent a few moments talking to a doctor. "So, he confirmed there was a liver puncture from the fall, but they were able to find the source of the bleeding and stop it. He said there doesn't look to be any brain trauma, but there is a bit of swelling, so he is in a medically induced coma to monitor his brain activity and to allow it to go down on its own. I also want to clarify that he wasn't fully extended in the picker; he had lowered it after the first explosion when I was already on my ass. It was about 10 to 15 feet in the air, not 30 feet at full extension. But he did break his arm and fractured his elbow, both on the same arm. I'm not sure if that's lucky or unlucky."

I felt so much at ease but realized that his injuries would require a lot of help. He would have to get used to using his good arm and possibly changing his dexterity until he healed.

I was so deep in thought on the car ride, thinking about what I could do, that I didn't realize I was home until Kelly said something.

They dropped me off and told me they would return in half an hour. Angellica was waiting in her car, promptly followed me in, and got comfortable on the couch with her pillow and blanket. It was a tad chilly, so I grabbed the heavier blankets to recreate the blanket bed near the dark fireplace. I could tell Angellica wanted to ask me if I was okay, but I tried to keep busy as I sniffled while putting everything together.

"I'm going to whip something up for the group. Let me know if you need help with anything. I'm here for you, Livi. She flips on the TV as the news reports on the fire and how they were just now getting it under control with local and two neighboring companies. They aren't sure of the cause yet but suspect improper chemical storage as one possibility. They replay footage caught on camera of the first explosion, then back to real-time as they pan over to show the truck on its side, the cabin smashed to pieces. The fire chief reports several serious injuries and one critical injury to his employee manning the cabin hose.

Nick. He was the only one critically injured. My emotions were all over the place; I couldn't listen anymore. I ran upstairs to my room; the tears fell before I could even close the door. I wiped them away and walked toward the window. I lean against my bedroom windowsill and hold myself. There was a lone light on; Beck must be there. His house and mine are plunged into a sea of darkness, and I can't take it. I want to showcase the whimsical nature of our favorite holiday. It's how we met, in a tense but flirtatious exchange about dominating and winning the town's competition. From there, it grew to something more, an undeniable attraction, or at least that's how I feel.

I change into a simple gown and robe, then return downstairs to turn on my lights. I looked back to see that everyone was watching me. "He would want his lights on, too. Beck, could you?"

I sit facing the window, watching Beck trudge over and into the house and then his beautiful homage shined brightly. I know he couldn't see it, but I hope he felt it in some way. That his love of his family would help bring him back to me. That, maybe, they were telling him not yet and that he had so much more to do here with me.

There are a lot of things I was hoping for. I hoped he would forgive me for flying off the handle and overreacting. I hoped he would ask me to be his girlfriend and we would make each other happy in time.

"Brr! It is frigid out there without my fire gear. This is why I don't go outside unless you send me out for errands or firewood."

"Speaking of firewood, can you light the fireplace for us, please?" Kelly bats her eyelashes, and he gives in.

He kissed her temple, "Of course, honey. I can't have my lady and my baby freeze. Now to navigate with a broken arm."

Angellica finishes up what looks like warm, gooey sandwiches and goes searching in my cabinets. I take a wild guess, "Chips are in the pantry, three kinds." She gives me a thumbs up.

Kelly plops down next to me, "I want you to eat something, then get some sleep. You've been through a pretty traumatic experience."

"My adrenaline is still going; I feel like I could stay awake for another 12 hours."

She looks at Beck, and they nod, "That means you're going to crash hard as you settle down. Why don't you find a holiday movie for us to watch? You know they're playing 24 hours of A Christmas Story and Miracle on 34th Street."

I was a sucker for A Christmas Story; it was my go-to and always made me feel joyous and festive; I hoped it would work its magic. I tune in and Angel hands me a plate. It was a Monte Cristo sandwich and some sour cream and cheddar chips.

"Thank you." I could feel my body start to slow down and feel extremely drowsy. I hope to have sweet dreams of us.

"Anything else, ladies?" I barely heard Beck ask.

"Here, two Monte Crisco sandwiches and chips. You want anything to drink?" He took the plate from Angel and smiled, "I'm good. My boy has a great selection of alcohol. You ladies need me; you know where to find me." He kissed Kelly on the forehead and tried to kiss her stomach, but she blocked him, squealing.

I was the first to get up the next morning. I couldn't fully rest knowing he was alone in the hospital. I was going down there the moment it was available to visitors. He wasn't going to spend Christmas alone. I made myself a travel mug of coffee and left a note of where I was. I changed to something comfortable and packed a small bag of supplies, a few bottles of water, and snacks. One chunky scarf and coat later, I was on my way.

"Good morning. Who are you here to see?" The nurse at reception asked me.

"Morning, Nick Nicholas, he's a firefighter who came in last night."

She checks her clipboard, "Okay, he's out of ICU and down the hall in room 334. He may still be unconscious, but he's out of danger."

"Thank you. Merry Christmas." It sounded sadder than I meant it, but I wanted her to know she and the other staff were appreciated for working during the holidays.

My ears picked up on steady beeps, and it got louder because his door was open. My hands were shaking because I knew he was hurt badly by the news report, but I didn't know it was this bad. It caused a hard stop. He was asleep, but there were so many tubes and machines he looked like he was at death's door.

"It looks worse than it is, I promise you." A voice says, startling me. Then, I see a young nurse looking at all the machines.

"I'm Colby, Mr. Nicholas' day nurse, and Clara is his night shift nurse. Our info is on that board if you need us or have questions."

I'm still stuck in that spot: "When will he wake up? And when can he go home?"

"He could wake up at any time now. He was given a low dosage to keep him sedated after the surgery, but the swelling has gone down substantially. We can still monitor his conscious state. He may have difficulty speaking at first or slurring, but it's temporary; the breathing tube does that. We'll run a battery of tests once he's awake and if everything is optimal, he'll go home with a mobile rehab service schedule. He'll need rehab for at least 12 weeks, and it'll be best if someone is available for at least the first two weeks."

I had sat down and taken his hand, squeezing while brushing his hair away. "I live next door. I'll take care of him."

"That's good. Looks like he'll be in good hands. I'll check back in a few hours."

"Thank you, Colby. I'm Elivia."

When he walked out, the silence was deafening. I took his hand in both of mine and kissed it. "Merry Christmas, Mr. Claus. I hope you can hear me, Nick. Please wake up." I laid my head on our adjoined hands. I said a little prayer before I turned on his TV to drown out the machine noises. I went to the blinds and opened them a bit and was surprised to see flurries! They were falling at a decent rate. I guess I wouldn't mind getting snowed in here. It's not like my fantasy, but I was content as long as I was with him.

"Is this how you imagined spending our first Christmas together? It definitely wasn't on my bingo card." I choked up and let the tears fall in a laughter/heartbreak combination. I hold myself while watching the area become a winter wonderland, glancing back to see his eyes hopefully. I took the remote and tried to find something whimsical. I found Home Alone playing and curled up in the recliner in the corner with my blanket and an extra hospital pillow. I plugged in my phone and drifted off to sleep.

Wake up, Mrs. Claus... you have to wake up...

I'm startled out of my sleep when I remember where I am. I swore he told me to wake up, but it was just my overactive and hopeful imagination. He was still lying there unconscious. I took the time to check my phone and saw three calls each from the girls, then texts from them asking if I needed anything. I assured them I was okay. It was close to lunch, so I made my way down to the cafeteria to grab something quick and not break into my stash. I got a nice ham and cheese sandwich, went to the salad bar to grab lettuce, onion, and jalapenos, gave it a squirt of spicy mustard and some chips, then returned; I didn't want to be away too long.

A bit later, Colby came back in for his rounds. "How are you holding up?"

"I wish for more comfortable chairs, but nothing can be done about that. Otherwise, I'm just hopeful; my Christmas wish is for him to wake up."

He replaces one of his IV bags, "So, are you guys...together? I sense way more than the friendly neighbor vibe." He motions between us with a big smile.

I chuckle, "That is a very complicated story."

"Perhaps another time. How about I bring in another bed so you can lay beside him if you decide to stay over, which, judging by the time you seem to be leaning towards."

"I can do that?" He looks around, placing his finger over his lips, "I'll leave a little note. Sometimes, we allow patients one overnight visitor. And you seem so determined to be the first thing he sees, and I might be a sucker for a good love story, so yes. I'll bring you one from maternity; they're cushier."

"Thanks so much."

A few minutes later, he activates the double door and carts in the bed with a little surprise. It was a mini decorated tree!

"This is my last-minute attempt to brighten your holiday. It sucks to have to spend it in the hospital. It plays the 12 Days of Christmas; also, I put together a little bag. It's got red and green popcorn, some gingerbread men, and I may

or may not have snuck in a mini bottle of Bailey's for some hot chocolate."

"You are my favorite Christmas elf right now!" He sets it all up and I threw my blanket and provisions in the bed when there was a tap on the glass. It was Kels, Beck, and Angel. I figured they'd come by eventually; I practically left them at my house.

"Hey sweetie, how are you? I see you got quite the setup. Any improvement?"

"Colby just brought me the bed. I had been in the recliner earlier. He said I could stay over if I wanted. I have everything I need to do that. Nothing's changed yet. I keep squeezing his hand and whispering that I'm here. I don't know what else I can do."

"I think you're doing enough. We wanted to lay eyes on both of you and..." Beck and Angellica pull containers from behind their backs. "To have Christmas dinner together. I knew you wouldn't come back to the house."

It looks like they got all the trimmings, and even though chicken noodle soup is delicious, it doesn't compare to a traditional dinner.

"Where did you guys get all this? I thought the store was closed."

Kelly sat in the recliner while they started fixing plates. "Beck and I had a small dinner set up and Angellica rounded out the rest to make enough for all of us."

Angel opens up the container of gravy to pour over the turkey. "Yeah, I was planning to eat alone as usual, but this is much better. Kind of feels like family." She hands me a plate and takes up the regular chair. Beck shares the extra bed with me. I think we all said a silent prayer over the food and his health. I started to hyper-focus on the beeps again, so I found one of the classics on TV.

At the end of the movie, they started to sing the 12 Days of Christmas and we took it as a challenge. I remembered my gift from Colby and used the whimsical little tree to keep it authentic, except you have to press it after every refrain.

We got the first five verses down easily, but most people can sing those with no problem. After that, it got harder to recall, and we sounded like a train wreck while the tree taunted us with its steady tune, pressuring us to keep up.

On the seventh day of Christmas, my true love sent to me... 7 Swans a Swimming, 6 Geese a Laying, 5 Golden Riiiiiiiiiiings... 4 Calling Birds, 3 French Hens, 2 Turtle Doves, and a Partridge in a Pear Tree!

We all giggle before attempting the next refrain. It truly was the joy I needed right now.

"Alright, next verse!"

On the eighth day of Christmas, my true love sent to me...

Then there was silence, deafening silence. "Oh my god, it's uhhh...it's eight...I don't know!" We all look at each other. The tree continued on without us as we struggled.

Angellica gasps, "I'll look it up!"

"Ei...eight maids a...milking." A raspy voice said before coughing and all eyes looked over immediately.

"Nicky!" I screamed, and then I slammed my lips against his in excitement. I gasp and pull back, feeling the blush on my cheeks.

Mental note: I have never called him that before. Where did that come from? It's cute, I like it.

He groaned, "Oh, brother and hello to you, too." He coughs and I grab the water and straw. He takes a tiny sip and looks at all the faces staring at him.

"Stop staring at me. I'm fine. I heard the most beautiful voice telling me to come back." He smiled at me, raised his good hand, and I took it. We look at each other until, "Oh, for the love of Pete. Could you not be so...nauseatingly sweet? Gag! They're already making out in front of us." Kelly dry heaves but smiles. "How are you feeling, Nick?"

"Sore, definitely sore. My chest hurts and my arm is numb as shit. I can't feel it. I guess that's a good thing. Beck, I think I'll be out of commission for a while."

"It's okay, buddy, me too." Beck turns so Nick can see his cast and he laughs, "You focus on getting healed. I'll call and let them know you're awake. I'm sure everyone wants to come see you."

Nick sniffs the air, trying to pinpoint something. "Something smells amazing. What day is it?"

"It's Christmas and they brought dinner to me because I was going to spend Christmas with you."

"I suppose that would make my stay a bit more tolerable."

"Did you really hear me?"

"Not only that, but I also dreamt of you too and how I would make all of this right. I'm sorry."

I shook my head, "You have nothing to be sorry for. I overreacted; my disguise wasn't as good as I had hoped." I see the girls nod their heads.

He pulls my hand to his lips, "Still the prettiest girl I've seen. Hand me the bed remote, will you, or prop me up. This flat view is boring. Besides, I'm starving."

"I don't think you're allowed regular food yet."

"Oh, come on, it's Christmas. You wouldn't let Santa starve, would you?" He's laying it on thick. "Let me buzz Colby before his shift ends and I'll prop you up. Let me know if there's any pain."

"You know my nurse by name, huh? Interesting..." He says and I know what he was implying, so I ignore him. I hit the call button and then slowly raised the head of the bed. I didn't want him fully upright with his bad arm, so I had him close to 45 degrees, enough to see around the room. Colby comes in as I set the remote down.

"Mr. Nicholas, good to see you awake and alert. My name is Colby."

"So, I've heard." He remarked snidely.

Colby also ignores him and checks his vitals. "Your Christmas angel there was not going to leave your side. You treat her well; she's already become one of my favorite people."

"Aww, thanks. So, the question is, is he allowed to have regular food yet? We have dinner here." He looks at the spread of turkey, mac and cheese, mashed potatoes, green beans, and rolls. He taps his cheek while contemplating, "Your stomach might be sensitive due to the medications, but this seems similar to what we would serve for the holidays, but this looks way better than processed turkey cubes in lumpy gravy. It should be okay. I will bring some ginger ale and some Alka seltzer if it isn't. Slow and small bites, Mr. Nicholas." He states sternly as Kelly starts his small plate.

I saw Angellica get kind of fidgety the moment Colby walked in. He was a handsome young man around her age. He was tall with blonde hair. He reminded me of a college football player. Not sure if there is a college nearby.

Anyway, she straightened up and cleared her throat, "Umm, Colby? We have extra. Would you like a plate to take home, so you don't have to eat gross hospital food?" She pushes her glasses up. I witnessed the moment he turned in her direction, noticed her, and this smile formed. It was that flirtatious type of smile.

"I get off in ten minutes. Would you have this with me in the cafeteria?" He holds out his hand and she realizes it was an open-ended question, but she squeaks awkwardly. She looks at me, panicked for help.

I break up the awkwardness, "Colby, this is Angellica, and she would love to have dinner with you. Go on now!" Kelly loads up his plate, and she practically pushes them and their plates out the door.

She squeals loudly, "Oh my gosh, how cute were they?!" Beck comes back in, "Who was that guy? Where were they going?" Kelly fills him in to keep him calm. He was starting to go into protective big brother mode.

22

NICK

I thought I was dreaming about my family singing the 12 Days of Christmas until they faded away, and suddenly, I was opening my eyes to find out who was singing...rather butchering my favorite song.

Nothing was more beautiful than seeing her smile as they sang. Until they got stuck, she looked so relieved to see me. That kiss was electric and surprising. She screamed out Nicky, relieved to see my eyes looking back at her. She has never called me anything besides Nick, Santa, or my favorite, St. Nick. I cringed hearing my childhood nickname, but right now, she can call me whatever she wants as long as she calls me hers.

"Hey." I feel her squeeze my hand as the plate is set before me. "Do you want me to..." She motions toward the plate, hinting if I wanted her help.

As much as I would love that, I need to see my range of motion. I slowly reached for the plastic fork, way slower than normal, but I expected that. I got a firm grip, and she pushed the plate closer. The potatoes felt like cement, and I couldn't lift them too far from the plate. I conceded and she took over. I sighed in frustration.

"Hey. It's okay. I don't mind being your nurse." My perverted mind races with images of her in a sexy nurse's outfit and I think she noticed. "Really?"

"What can I say? I have a super-hot nurse. She feeds me and I look forward to a very intimate sponge bath. Because of your old...job, what are the chances you actually have a hot nurse outfit?"

We were in our own little bubble. I could see she was going to answer my inquiry before someone cleared their throat, and I saw Beck and Kelly. "We're still here but won't cramp your space for much longer."

Beck sits on the edge of my bed; Livi sits back, breaking up our intimate moment. "Tell me, what do you remember before the truck fell?"

That was a good question. It all happened so quickly. "I remember the flash of the first explosion, which shook the whole truck. At that moment, I wondered if we had lowered the stabilizers and the horror in realizing we hadn't due to the fast pace and severity of the scene. We were complacent. Then the second explosion and the freefall, I think, was the worst part. I blacked out; I don't even remember feeling the impact. Or maybe the impact caused the blackout; either way, I don't remember. I suppose that's a plus. I recall being in my thoughts, my memories. Then waking up." I opened my mouth like a baby bird to receive the mashed potatoes I had been salivating for and they tasted extra garlic buttery.

Everyone eats while Livi pulls double duty feeding herself and me, but she only smiles and giggles like a schoolgirl whenever our eyes meet.

"Is this all it took to have you all to myself? Plummeting to the Earth with a few scrapes and bruises?" I smiled, but she didn't; she frowned and set down the fork. I saw her breathing hitch as if she was trying not to cry. "Hey hey hey, I'm sorry. It was a bad joke."

She quickly wiped away a stray tear, "It was a terrible joke! You could have died! And you have way more than a few scrapes and bruises!" I recalled what had happened to her father. She was reliving her most traumatic memory. "Come here. I'm so sorry. I forgot about what happened to your father. I didn't mean to joke. It won't happen again." She leans down, resting her head on my chest, and I kiss her forehead. She's quiet as she clutches my hospital gown. The only sound is that of the TV.

A few minutes later, I was still scratching her scalp. Kelly got my attention, "We're going to go."

I nod, "Is she asleep?"

"Yeah, the poor thing was so worried about you. You got something special here, Nicky."

"Not you, too." That nickname is going to stick.

She fluffs my hair, "We'll check in with her later. See you tomorrow and Merry Christmas."

"Merry Christmas." Not the one I planned, but she's in my arms, and that's enough. I turned the volume down and glanced out the window; it was a steady shower of flurries. What if she gets snowed in? She should go home.

"Livi, wake up." She groans and slides her arm around my waist, squeezing a bit, but doesn't wake up. I'm thankful it wasn't my freshly operated side. I lift up my good side a bit, then drop it to shake her awake. She inhales and rubs her eyes. "It's snowing pretty heavily. You should go and sleep in your own bed."

"Noooo. I have all I need here...to stay over. Comfortable." She utters before she nods back off. What a good way to end Christmas, even if it's all banged up in the hospital.

My night nurse came to check on me, but I didn't want to disturb her sleep. "I'll check back at 5 a.m. or so. She looks exhausted but also happy. You buzz me if you need pain relievers or anything."

"I will," I whisper as I inhale her soft, sweet scent and fall asleep happily.

Later, I woke up with my arm on fire. The pain was excruciating. My grunts and labored breathing woke her up.

She shot up fast, "Did I hurt you?! Oh my god, you're sweating so much!"

"Page the nurse; pain is unbearable." She pressed it and she came in promptly with her cart. "You're overdue for a dose. On a scale of one to ten, what's your pain level?"

"Solid fucking 30!"

"Alright, we'll do a straight shot in the arm this time for quicker relief, and in eight to ten hours, we'll do the intravenous way when it starts to wear off. Now, it will burn and temporarily worsen it before it gets better. Should only be a few minutes."

She pulls out this ginormous needle. Did I mention I hate needles? I looked away to see Elivia had moved to the other side.

"Full name." The nurse says, but it didn't register.

"What?"

"State your full name."

"Nick Saint Nicholas." I see her trying to suppress her laughing. "What's so funny?"

"It's so fitting."

"Alright, all done. That was enough of a distraction."

She was not kidding. It was a burning sensation all over and then a stinging. Moments later, it started to subside, and I sighed loudly in relief. Livi wipes the sweat away.

After the nurse leaves, she laughs, "Is that why you liked to hear me call you St. Nick when...I cum? You know this increases your perversion quotient exponentially." The way her tone dropped to a sexy whisper, I may be injured, but I felt that all the way down.

"Perhaps, but I believe you enjoyed it as much as me, Mrs. Claus. I was the one drowning in your milk and cookies."

She bit her lip before she shifted a bit, "I'm glad that Mr. Claus is finally resting on Christmas."

"But who delivered all the gifts to the boys and girls?"

She ponders for a moment, "Oh, the Santa bot I ordered."

"Clever girl. Are you sure you want to stay over? I won't think any less if you want the comfort of your bed."

She sighs, but it sounds like a moan, "My bed is comfy, you know that, but no, I wouldn't sleep. I could barely sleep last night, so I was here right at visiting hours. I didn't know how bad it was because they wheeled you right into surgery, and Beck stayed at your place." She looked away to give herself a moment. She broke the silence by climbing back on the other side, resuming her grip around my waist.

"So now I'm curious, what's your full name? Since I gave you such a laugh."

"It's Elivia Noelle Winters."

"It's beautiful. Apparently, I'm not the only one with a holiday-themed name." I kissed her forehead, "Get some rest."

"Okay. Merry Christmas, Nick."

"Merry Christmas, Elivia."

23

ELIVIA

It's been three days. That's how much time has passed since my sleepover in his hospital room. Now, he was being released. Beck and his crew visited him the day after Christmas. Many of them were surprised to see me there, and I'm sure they teased him after I left them to have their guy time. They also went to his house to set up one of his guest bedrooms so that he could avoid the stairs for a while. He can walk around, but he's still sore and slow.

Work has kept me occupied but getting random updates from Beck during the lulls helped. He definitely doesn't know how to set up a bedroom; he sent me a picture of a sheet set asking which sheet goes first, the scrunchy one, as he called it, or the straight one. He also asked whether a sham was the same as a pillowcase. I haven't had a good laugh in a long time. I would double-check their work before Nick gets home, which should be soon, maybe even today!

My phone buzzed, but I didn't recognize the number.

Unknown number: Hello, beautiful

I wondered if it was Xav from another number since I blocked the main one. After the kick to his manhood, it should be super clear that he had no chance, but he was arrogant and would still be bold enough to try.

Me: Who the hell is this?

Unknown: It's Nick. Beck brought me my phone and charger and gave me your number.

Me: Oh! Sorry.

Nick: You sound annoyed or upset.

Me: I didn't want to deal with Xavier or his BS. I feel stupid and naive that everyone saw through his game except me.

Nick: He's a snake in the grass and charming. I'm glad you see it now, and I don't have to dismember his body for lying on me.

Me: Wow, dismemberment. Such appealing qualities. I don't want to talk about him with you.

Nick: I agree. I'm being released today; Beck is coming to pick me up now.

Me: Awesome, I think they finished prepping your temporary room.

He was silent for a minute, and then the text bubbles flashed while he was typing.

Nick: Will you come by?

Me: Of course, I'll even cook dinner. You are my sole responsibility for the next two weeks.

Nick: What about the shop?

Me: We close for New Year's Eve and Day. It'll be slow up until then and Angellica will call me if she needs me to come in. In fact, she insisted.

As we are texting, I whisper to Angellica about his release. She smiles, giving me a thumbs up. I grab my things from the office and Colby is at the counter with food when I come out. He's leaned over super close to her.

"Hey Colby, nice to see you!" I said in a teasing tone. They are so cute! It's super sweet...wait, is this what Kelly meant about Nick and me?

"You, too. Just bringing Angel lunch."

"That's adorable. Well, they released Nick. I'm going to the house to double-check everything's in order."

"Oh, that's good to hear Mr. Nicholas is being released. We had a nice long conversation yesterday." There was that mischievous smile again, and Angellica gave me the same smile. Obviously, they had been talking since their impromptu date, and I have a feeling I was a part of their conversation.

"Tell Nick I said hi! Let me know if you need me to whip up dinner and drop by."

"Thanks...Angel. I have dinner for tonight. Perhaps you can whip up something ...for the both of you...you know, at your house." She blushed when I pointed at both of them and implied.

I wave at them as I head home. I park quickly and see a couple of cars there. Not sure who, though, but I did notice his decorations were taken down. I knock and walk in, "Hello, anybody there?"

Oh my, his house is breathtaking. It was above how I would expect a bachelor to decorate his home. He had a great eye for it, pairing warm browns with rich mahoganies with accents of black and white. I would swear his mother helped decorate the entire space had she not passed on. It felt very warm and welcoming.

Sure enough, as I'm walking in, a guy peeks his head from one of the rooms.

"Oh, Elivia, hey!" It was Jackson.

"Can I come back? I wanted to make sure Beck put the bedding on correctly. His text gave me anxiety." He waved me back and stood at the entrance. Jackson and Perry looked so proud of themselves, but their excitement quickly changed when they looked at my reaction...or lack thereof.

"No! It's not bad; it only needs a few more items. You guys did a decent job. Now, take down this list. If you need me to pay, I will. I need one body pillow, two more firm regular pillows, make sure they are firm, and a bunch of tank tops. Check his closet for the proper size. Oh, and snacks that can go in the room. Thank you, boys."

"I can tell Nick's going to be in very good hands," Perry says as he elbows Jackson, who agrees.

They chuckled on the way out and I knew what he was saying. I go to fluff the pillows and make it seem more welcoming when I see them in the corner. I didn't even think about the contest results since the explosion, but I'm now looking at the grand prize trophy and first-place ribbon. He won, and they nonchalantly shoved it into his guest room. No, it should be showcased proudly. After finishing his room, I took the trophy and ribbon to the living room. He had cream furniture with black and wood accents. He had a mantle with pictures of his beloved parents. Even their pictures radiated a love so pure and a bit of silliness with their ugly sweater photo. I placed the trophy on the floor since it was so large, but I pinned the ribbon to its frame. Now, it was properly displayed.

I checked his fridge and made a list, then tackled the dishes. It's like a fraternity threw a weekend summer bash here, minus beer cans everywhere, but I'd have to check every room to be sure.

"Honey, I'm home." Then I heard laughing as I made my way back to the front. Nick was standing pretty normally, but his arm was cast and bandaged. I would need to get plastic bags from my house for showers.

I held my arms up, then dropped them when I was in front of him. I thought it would be awkward in Beck's presence. Beck grinned, but Nick grabbed my hand and pulled me closer, "How about a welcome home kiss right here." He pointed to his cheek.

I leaned forward and kissed him gently. He's all smiles when I back away. "Welcome home."

Nick

"WELCOME HOME." She says after giving me such a sweet kiss. I didn't expect her to actually do it, but she did, and she lingered longer than expected.

She is absolutely beautiful.

"Thank you, sweetie. Beck, thanks for watching the place, and Livia, I appreciate you cleaning it up."

She was shocked, "How did you know?"

"I work with a bunch of slobs. It's like living in a frat house with them at the station. I know for a fact it wasn't this guy. He doesn't even know where I keep my cleaning supplies." She laughs, but he looks offended.

"Hey, I wasn't that messy. Tell him. Livi?!"

"Beck, you're a pig." Now we're both laughing, and he scoffs.

"Whatever. Do you need anything else from me? Kelly is asking for me to pick up lasagna, cottage cheese, ranch Doritos, and umm...grape jelly."

Well, it almost sounded normal.

He looked like he was nauseous just saying it, but she was carrying his child.

"Nothing from me. I sent Jackson and Perry for a few things and I'm going to start on dinner." Beck hands her my grocery bag full of meds, supplies, and instructions. "Call me if you need anything." And he waves us goodbye. The door closed and it was quiet until she hefted the bag and went to my guest bedroom. I followed her slowly. I was still sore where the incision was. I'd have to be extra cognizant to avoid a tear, although I am heavily bandaged.

She opens the bag and sets the bottles out on the dresser, reading each one out loud and setting them in order of frequency. She froze up when I was finally behind her, breathing heavily. "You smell so good." She turned around and our lips were so close.

"Nick..." She's lucky I don't have two good arms. I'd whisk her to my room and lock her in. I guess this temporary room will do.

She snapped out of our intense moment, "Oh! I have to show you something. Come on!"

Fighting my raging boner, I followed her into the living room. She pulls me in front of the mantle, but I'm too busy gazing at her.

"Look at your parent's picture." I see the first-place prize ribbon, then look down to see the trophy.

"I won...wow." I literally had no words.

"They set it in your temporary room, but I thought it would look better here and besides, they were the sole reason, and it should be properly displayed."

I won our title back and paid homage to the people who created me and loved each other conditionally and I couldn't be happier. That is until I remembered what I said. I wanted to take her in front of the trophy, to hear her moaning my name and claiming both my prizes, but now isn't the time.

The electricity was in the air.

"Well, I should get dinner started." She quickly put space between us as I turned on the TV.

"Alright folks, we may have had a fluke of a mild winter up until Christmas, but Santa brought us a hail Mary. That's right, an arctic front is coming from Canada on the way, and it will drop feet of snow, not inches. There's still a few hours left to gather supplies..."

I was going to walk back, but she was watching near the kitchen.

"What do we do? I can grab some clothes and food from my house. Yeah, I'll go do that..." She was going to walk past, but I stopped her. "No, we'll go to your house. You have the fireplace in case we lose power, and I can guarantee your fridge is fuller than mine."

"But I sent them to get the provisions you need."

"We'll take it over there. I'll pack clothes and my meds. You take whatever bedding I'll need. There's an hour or so of light outside; we can make a few trips."

I can see her little brain running a mile a minute. I pull her in with a kiss, "It'll be alright." That seemed to work as she grabbed pillows and placed them in the middle of the comforter, folding them up like a hobo bag. She hefted it and it almost took her down. She gained her balance and walked out.

In the coat closet was my duffle bag and I saw what clothes they placed down in the temporary room. I lucked out because they grabbed most of my underwear, sweats, and tank tops and although it's winter, I can't wear any sleeves with this cast. I pack the toiletries they put in the guest bath and hear her open the door.

"You good, Livi? It took you a bit longer than I expected."

"Yeah...I...brought some firewood inside the house. I didn't know how much, but I took in a handful. You can tell me once we're over there if it's enough. What can I take next?"

I thought and a devious game came to mind, "Can you go upstairs and grab my robe, razor, and condoms...top bedside drawer." I raised my brow to gauge her reaction. She scoffed, "I'll grab your robe and razor..." She steps super close; I can feel her breath on my lips. "Since when did we use those?" She grinned as she stepped away.

"Anything else?"

"Uh, they didn't bring down s-socks. You can look around and see if there's anything else up there."

I wasn't ready for her answer; I wanted to see her reaction to my boldness, and she countered with an even bolder statement. It's going to be an interesting few days. I heard her go up the stairs, and I continued packing. I turned off all the lights downstairs. I slowly make my way to the living room, setting down my bag. I go into the kitchen, open one of those reusable bags and start loading it up with whatever I could find. I was interrupted by a knock.

"Hey, Elivia, we brought all the stuff on the list. Hey Nick, how are you feeling? Did you see we're about to get a shit ton of snow? You're lucky you don't have to cover the firehouse shoveling duties. Looks to me like you'll have your...hand full." Parker was so proud of his joke, I'll let it slide. It wasn't the first and won't be the last, especially when I return to the firehouse.

"Oh, you can take that stuff next door. We're going to brave the storm at her place."

"Okay, well, get better and call the station if you need anything. We better get back. We probably have to take inventory. You know he'll send us out even if it is snowing sideways. He loves his mini-fried apple pies. In fact, we better pick some up on the way back."

"Yeah. Thanks for picking up what she asked for and taking it over there."

"Yeah, seeing the little love nest will be nice." I picked up a pillow to chuck at Jackson's head, but Livi came down the stairs with a handful of stuff before I could.

"Oh! Hey guys, thanks so much; you can take it to my house."

I lowered the pillow, but she gave me a look. "What were you about to do?"

"Nothing." She steps toward me and is dangerously close again. "Are you sure?"

She kissed me quickly and I buckled, "They were teasing me about staying at your place."

"That's all? You need tougher skin. None of the girlfriends or wives made fun of me at the hospital; they were very supportive, even when I fainted and ended up in a hospital bed."

"You did what?" A little detail she forgot to mention when we were laid up together. Perhaps she didn't want me to worry.

She looked down, realizing she hadn't revealed that to me before and I quickly lifted her chin up, "You're okay, that's all that matters." She nods and looks around, spotting my bag of random food.

"Did you pack enough? My kitchen is nowhere near as bare as yours."

"Let's call it a stash of extra food. Oh, let me grab my 80-year-old bourbon. I guess I shouldn't grab any wine?" I taper off while smiling at her.

"Whatever."

It took two more trips, and we piled it all into her living room and kitchen. I decided to grab a few more logs in a few trips. I could only grab one at a time.

_____

24

ELIVIA

I didn't notice until he came in a second time that he was adding to the log pile with his good arm.

"Nick, please sit down and rest. I'll grab a few more handfuls. It's time you took your meds, I put the bottles in the half bathroom."

I grab my coat and make two additional trips and carry as much as I can. By the second trip, he was kneeling at the fireplace, placing the logs carefully.

"I can do that, too. Why won't you rest?"

"Because darlin', you can't do it all. You'll work yourself to exhaustion. I have a bum arm and a slower stride, but I'm not helpless. Let me help set up before the storm. Last I checked, Santa and Mrs. Claus were a team."

Oh, *deer*. See what I did there? What is he doing to me?!

"Okay, but please take it easy. I will add your food to the pantry and start dinner. We're having Cajun pasta and garlic bread."

When I turned, I felt a smack and saw him stare, but there was a fire behind it. "Are you going to feed me? I already know what I want for dessert." He turns away adding another log to the fireplace. He knew the damage was done.

My legs were a little wobbly as the pain from that smack went straight to my core. I peek over at him tending to the fire, then he goes to take his meds in the bathroom. I can hear the bottles rattle.

"Hey, where do you want me to put my clothes?" That was a good question. "I need to clear a drawer for you and set up the bed."

"We can build our blanket fort again here and watch the snowfall. It'll be romantic like those movies on TV."

What does he know about that?

"Can you grab the candles and flashlights from this closet and place them on the side table? Just in case." I saw movement and then turned to focus on putting the pasta in the boiling water. I heard the TV turn on.

"It is picking up out there, folks." The meteorologist states as Nick wobbled past me, heading towards the stairs. "Excuse you, where are you going? I don't think you should be exerting that much on your body right now."

Then he attacks my neck, wrapping his arm around me as I fry the garlic in the pan before adding the basil and sauce.

"I think someone forgot who is in charge here. Don't worry about me. I'm grabbing the stuff for our bed fort. I think I can handle some blankets and pillows."

"What makes you think all that stuff is up there? We have your bedding, and the thick comforters are in the coat closet right there." I point to the closet by the front door.

"Yeah, but the ones up there are soaked in your essence, and I want you all over me...in every way."

Oh, sweet season's greetings.

Good grief, he's such a tease. I don't say anything and concentrate on dinner. I let Mr. Dominant do whatever he wants as I hear the stairs creak as he makes his way to my room.

I pour the pasta out from the pot into the saucepan and add the sauce, complete with shrimp, sausage, and a bit of truffle salt, then I put it on a low simmer. I place the garlic bread in the preheated oven and finish putting the groceries in the kitchen away. It was getting toasty with cooking and the fireplace roaring. From the kitchen window, I see the snow blanketing everything it touches and the wind picking up, whipping it all around.

Nick finally makes his way down with my bedding, including my pillows. He was pretty strong to only have the use of one arm. He locked eyes as he leaned into them and inhaled deeply. He started putting together our setup while I fixed the pasta bowls.

He started with the heavy comforters from the closet; I had two, and they would cushion us from the hard floor. Then he layered his blankets, then finally, mine. The whole spread covered the floor from couch to couch, a king-size area. Then he took the new body pillow and placed it vertically and off to the side, then piled the other pillows. It was super thick and full like we were sleeping on a cloud.

"Winter lovers rejoice! We will be broadcasting nonstop until this storm blows over. There is a decent chance that it could stall over parts of Northeast Ohio, stretching down West Pennsylvania to parts of West Virginia. I hope you're prepared because this could keep you indoors for a few days." He lowers the volume back.

"Crazy, huh? Glad we decided to hole up here."

"You don't think your place was up to the job?"

"It's not that. It's a lot of house; at least here, it's warm and cozy and the perfect setup. All we have to do is shift the tree to the side and have a prime view of the winter festivities."

I hear his slow steps come behind me and when I turn around, he has me caged in against the stove. "Perfect setup for what?"

"The perfect amount of space for me to take you on every square inch of this surface."

I swallow hard, then shove him playfully, "You're a sex-driven pervert."

"Well, before you, it had been a while."

"Hmm. Just you and your hand, huh?" I retort while laughing, putting our bowls on the placemats.

"Yeah, well, guys don't get the luxury of handheld toys like you girls do."

I gasped in horror. He didn't...did he? He was upstairs for a while, but it never crossed my mind. I thought he was taking his time so as not to injure himself more.

He paced behind me, "So, tell me, Mrs. Claus, is your little buddy in your shower cause for concern? I'll admit he looks quite impressive." He raised his brow, and my jaw dropped. I squeaked. Like a chew toy and shook my head.

"Good girl, I'd hate to be jealous of an inanimate object that has gotten you off more times than I have. It'd be a shame if he...disappeared."

"You touch Tony, you die! Now, enough about why you were snooping in my bathroom. Let's eat."

Nick

SHE COOKED the most delicious meal. We sat at the island and talked about random stuff, figuring out what we had in common. Who knew she liked to watch anime and cartoons like I do? Afterward, I helped as best I could as she cleaned up. I cleared out the dishwasher while she washed the dishes. The lights flickered, bringing the concern of a power outage back to the forefront.

"Hey, why don't you take a shower before the lights go out. It's been a long day and I know you're tired."

"Are you going to spy on me?" She looked back and smiled.

"Baby, if I wanted to watch you in the shower, I simply would. I'd pull up a chair and watch the soap slide over your skin as you scrub yourself clean, then I'd dry you off if I had two good hands. I really want you to settle down from the day while I take my next dose."

She eyed me and I held up the scout's honor signal and she chuckled while heading upstairs. The pain was starting to annoy me, so it was time for another dose because nothing would get in the way of pleasing her all night. I hear her shower going, down my pills and set up the living room for ambiance. I lit her holiday-scented candles and placed additional candles around the area if the lights went out. I placed some in the kitchen and two in the half bath. I light those and keep the door open. I also tossed a flashlight in there too. I put a lantern on the island and next to the fireplace, which was roaring nicely. Since we hadn't put up my clothes yet, I was able to change into my sleep pants and a tank top. I don't know why, but my pajama tops are in here. I can't even put one arm through; that would look weird. I tossed it on top of the bag. I think all the bedrooms are upstairs, so I put my bags against the wall and out of the way until the next time I can make it up there.

The news is reporting three inches of snow and counting, with snowfall for at least another 24 hours, if not more.

I hear the water stop and anticipate whatever piece of lingerie she decides to tease me with. I know Mrs. Claus would love to see my face when she pranced down.

I scan the channels and, thankfully find a Christmas movie playing. They usually don't stop the holiday showings until the new year. I can milk this Santa thing until then.

I find myself super tired after yawning and stretching.

Guess I was exhausted, too. It was hard to sleep, so they set my cast very early this morning. I take a closer look outside and my house looks hauntingly beautiful, the crisp whiteness of the snow blanketing my dark house. We were definitely going to be one of the last neighborhoods to get shoveled out.

I hear her coming down the stairs. "Hey, I found a Christmas movie we can…" I stop because she comes down the stairs in her underwear…just her underwear. A snow-white set, how can a color be so pure but also so dirty at the same time?

Sweet jingle bells…

She's smiling as she gets close. She puts an extra bounce in her step, making her tits jiggle so perfectly. Then she reaches down and slips my discarded sleep shirt over her body. It was oversized on her; she playfully buttoned two of them. So much skin was still showing.

"So, what do you think?" She does a cute little spin before leaning against me.

"I liked the first outfit, but this is a different kind of sexy. You lay claim by wearing half of my outfit. I like it. You packed my pajamas, didn't you?"

"May…be." She takes my hand, and we stand in front of the window. "Isn't it beautiful? It's another check marked off my wish list to be snowed in with a handsome man."

We stand in silence for a moment, then she yawns. "Time for bed."

"No, I'm fine, it's just…"

"Been a long day. You worked, then went to my house, cleaned, moved stuff from my house to yours, then put everything away, and cooked. It's time for bed, Elivia."

She was falling asleep against me, "That's Mrs. Claus to you." She said, so deliriously tired. I help her down and she snuggles up in the blanket and she's asleep in no time. She is stunning even when she's snoring. She's absolutely exhausted. She wasn't obligated to take care of me; she chose to, and I appreciate her for that, but I had a dream of my own, and I am starting to see her in such a different light. Seeing her as someone special and not just my flirtatious neighbor whose feistiness showed me different sides of her. I sat on the couch for a while as I watched her sleep.

After years of sad and failed misery, was it finally my time? I only wanted what my parents had, but then I put it in perspective that my story wasn't going to be exactly like theirs. That my heartbreak and seclusion, focusing on my career, was my own path until I saw that moving truck in the driveway.

I alternate looking at her and the snow falling outside. It went from slow fat flakes to a fury and blizzard-like. Now, it was starting to whip around in the viciousness of the wind. The trees were doing their best in these conditions. I hope they remained upright, so they didn't bring down any power lines.

"Nick..." I looked down and saw her looking at me.

"You're supposed to be sleeping," I tell her, but I'm actually glad she's awake.

I joined her in bed, laying on my good side, and although I could take her and dive deep into her sweet center, I found staring at her in silence speaks volumes. It's intense and it makes my entire body heat up.

Suddenly, we hear a pop, and her lights flicker before they go out.

"Oh...there goes the lights. Guess it was coming; I didn't think it would happen so soon. Thank goodness for battery banks. Can you switch the phones over, so they are still charging?" I unplug both from the outlet and then connect them to the battery pack. Picking her place was genius because I didn't have half of what she had.

I climb back into our bird's nest; I lay propped up on pillows against the couch. Elevated to keep the cast from applying pressure on my arm.

"Are you okay?"

"Yeah, I set up my side this way to sleep comfortably. I knew laying on my back wouldn't last long." She lays across my stomach and lap, putting her pillow underneath and I sigh in relief. There's still a chance she could feel me through the pillow. I'd been raging hard since she bounced down the stairs.

As I played in her hair, she exhaled hard, "Tell me about the big city living in New York."

She shot me a look as she now lay on her back. "Have you never left Asher Falls?"

"I've gone to Chicago for a firemen's convention and a few smaller places, but nothing compared to New York."

"You're right. Chicago is nothing compared to New York. Maybe you can come with Angellica and me when I take her to see the Macy's Christmas display." Her hands are now holding onto my arm that stretches across her chest.

"I'd like that, but what I want more is to share a kiss in the middle of that huge ice rink."

"Oh, the rink at Rockefeller Square. I never got to skate there myself."

"That doesn't even make sense. Why didn't you go?"

She sighs and sits up, "Once you become a model or spokesperson for some brand, your body is to be protected at all times. No physical activities outside of the gym. It was pretty much work, company events and nights at the bars with friends. Now I can do all the things I missed: ice skating, hiking, horseback riding. I want to finally live my life my way."

She laid back down and, in the silence, the firewood crackled. I would need to stoke the fire soon because it was starting to get chilly. I set her up and slide from underneath her, climb over her, and put another log on the fire, making sure the flames reach it. The flames now reached higher, and the heat radiated much more in our immediate space.

I resumed my place, and she stared so sweetly at me. Opening her heart without words. She signaled for a kiss, and I leaned down as much as I could, and she met me the rest of the way. One turned into a few, and the next thing I knew, she was straddling me. It was a scene right out of those Christmas movies before they faded to black for network television.

But then she leaned forward to lay against me, and I rubbed her back. These silent moments were eye-opening; we could enjoy the peace of each other.

"Tell me about your old job."

"Ahh, the glamorous life of modeling. Don't get me wrong, I loved my job. I actually enjoyed the time getting hair and makeup done, slipping on the sexiest lingerie, and posing for the world to see, but it became so monotonous like the rest of my life. I was bored and it became work. I guess I lost my passion and don't get me started on the dating scene. Pretentious assholes as far as the eye can see. For them, I was a trophy, the ability to say that they dated a model. Sometimes they said supermodel, but I wasn't. I wasn't even the type of model they were bragging about. They wanted Victoria's Secret-level lingerie models; I was nowhere near that caliber."

"You were to me. The only model in the catalog to rile me up, the only one in my fantasies and...the only one to umm..."

25

ELIVIA

He stopped mid-sentence, but I'm pretty sure I knew what he was about to say. I had to be sure, though. "Only one to what?" I rocked back and forth in his lap and saw him starting to get flustered, his good hand now on my hip, trying to coax him to continue.

"Livi..."

"Only one to what? Did you stroke yourself to me? Is that why the catalog is sitting on your nightstand? Why you were always peeking out your window? To watch me." He only nodded as I ground my hips deeper into him, feeling friction between us and I bit my lip to muffle a moan, but he groaned loudly, making me grind even faster. It started to feel so good. It was good enough for him to reach up and grab my throat.

"Oh...yesss...Nick..."

"Yes, you were the one I jerked off to. Your body, your smile, but those eyes sent me over as I imagined you calling my name when you shattered over me. When you actually did, it was way better than I could ever imagine and judging by the way you're grinding on me now, I might be able to coax another one out of you, hmm?" He raised his brow. He could have whatever he wanted. He squeezed my throat a bit and pulled me closer at the same time.

"You know Santa never got his after-Christmas gift. Rewarding him for all that hard work, flying all over the world, spreading happiness and joy. And the only thing he wanted was Mrs. Claus bent over the kitchen counter, but since I'm injured, I'll settle for you riding me to exhaustion. You know you want that, to cum all over my lap, then fall asleep in my arms."

It sounded like a dream to me. Snowed in, no electricity, and the only way to keep warm was mind-blowing sex with a hot firefighter? Sign me up.

I unbuttoned the button he'd been staring at, trying to will it to unfasten itself, but I finally put him out of his misery. I start to slide it off, but he slides it back on.

"Don't you dare take a single thing off. Oh no, Santa's going to claim you in his clothes." He told me and I nodded my compliance. His hand went up to my neck once more but slid down between my breasts that were pushed up so high. Of course, I chose it on purpose to tease, but it gave him more real estate to touch as he went down the middle, then squeezed each one and then the nipple, causing my core to throb in anticipation.

His hand continued down my stomach, and his fingers slipped underneath my underwear.

"My, my, my Mrs. Claus, you are ready, aren't you? How long has it been? I thought you'd at least use your shower buddy while I was out of commission."

Are you kidding me, Tony was child's play in comparison. He fell off as the main player to a supporting role. Nick's fingers found a pleasure point I never felt before, and I dug my nails into his shoulders, slamming my lips into his and moaning at the same time. He leaned back to separate us, "Oh no, Santa wants to hear from his good girl how good it feels. Tell me, Elivia...say it." He slowed his movement, making me frustrated. I tried to help by rocking faster, but then he stopped and then I stopped.

"Nick, please. Your fingers feel so good inside of me. I want more. I need it." I reach down between my legs to squeeze him. He was so hard.

"See what you do to me? As much as I'd like to draw this out all night," He released himself from his pajamas and I centered myself over and slid down.

The lights flickered but remained out, but I didn't care. I felt his hand on my hip before pushing me down every time I rose. It was more aggressive than usual, but I wasn't complaining.

"Fuck Livi, yes! You feel so good, such a tight and greedy little pussy. How does it feel, huh?" He licks his fingers previously inside me and circles my clit, sending shockwaves through my body. And that's all it took; my orgasm rushed forward so fast I was disappointed I couldn't prolong it.

"Oh, Nick!"

I lay panting on his chest, feeling the rumble from his chuckling. Then the burning sting of his hand on my ass, "On your knees. I'm glad you got yours, but we're not done yet."

I scrambled so quickly. "Lean against the couch, Mrs. Claus." I quickly correct myself and I feel him behind me. He slides my panties over and slides so slowly into me, pushing and pulling at a snail's pace. Until he wraps his hand in my hair, pulling me against him and slamming into me. "Oh God, yes!"

He's very aggressive to only have one good arm. I don't know if he was venting or proving he could still give me the time of my life. It didn't matter to me because I could feel another orgasm on the horizon.

"There, there! I'm gonna cum! Don't stop, don't stop, don't

stop!" I begged and he let me go and I lay against the couch, counter-thrusting, pushing against his movements. "Oh, baby, you take it. Take that dick, I feel you tightening so good. Oh yeah, you're going to make me explode. Are you going to cum for Santa? Be my little holiday slut! All he wanted for Christmas was to feel you." Then he leaned into me, biting my ear, and then whispering, "You better get my name right when you cum."

Oh, jingle bells.

I hope he doesn't continue this holiday fetish where I have to do this with every holiday. I'll concede to Christmas, Halloween, and even Thanksgiving because who doesn't love a good...stuffing. Okay, I admit it is kind of hot. No, what is he doing to me?! It didn't matter because his hand groped my breasts but also helped him slam into me. "I'm going to cum but not before you baby girl. I know you're close, Mrs. Claus. Oh yeah, tighten that little pussy around me."

I was so dizzy in pleasure that I let everything go, including a scream to rival a tea kettle.

"Ohhh! St. Nick!"

"That's it, baby! Grrrr!"

Did he just growl? He thrust forward one good time, laying me on the couch with him laying on top of me, but only until he realized. "Sorry. Are you okay?"

"Mhmm! We came at the same time. How's your arm?"

He winced, "I think it's time for a muscle relaxer, darlin'. I'm starting to feel that all too familiar burning sensation." I ran into the bathroom to grab it and then a glass of water. Now he's leaned against the couch with his pillows supporting his back.

"Here. Maybe we can put pillows under your cast to alleviate the pressure when you lie on your back. I can't imagine it being more comfortable propped up like that."

He tosses the pills and quickly washes them back with

water. "There is no comfort with a cast. It's okay; I don't mind spending my night watching you sleep."

I stack two, "Come on, let's try. Lay down." He lays down, the cast cushioned by the pillows.

"Can you put one under my lower back, please?" When I do, he sighs in relief. I took a moment to stoke the fire and then hid under the covers, cozied up to him because it was getting cold; all that built-up heat from sex was wearing off. I cover his cast and most of his chest before I lay slightly on top of him. His good arm wraps around me, and I feel his lips on my forehead.

"Are you cold?"

"Just a bit, but I'll be okay. We can add more firewood if need be. Or I can put on real clothes."

"Oh no, I'll lay on top of you before you change out of my clothes. It's so fucking hot."

His hand slides under me to shift himself. I shake my head, "You're a sex pervert, Mr. Claus."

"You don't have to continue; the holiday is over. You can call me Nick."

"I know, but it's kinda fun, it's our thing."

His hand that returned to my waist now squeezed me, "Ours?"

"Well, yeah. Is this the awkward pre-official conversation? Can we skip it? I don't have any rules or anything like that. We can do it day by day."

"You want to be my girl?"

"I mean, I could always go back to Xavier." I separate myself, but his hand catches me and pushes me further in. "You're asking for a spanking and not the good kind, either."

∼

Nick

HER FACE FELL when I threatened her with a punishment she couldn't get pleasure from. The room was quiet again except for the fire. She was staring right into my soul, and I was mesmerized. She leaned in slowly and kissed me. It was a peck, quick and innocent, feeling me out. Then the next one was a bit more intense as she let my tongue in, and her leg slid across my lap, teasing. She whimpered when I grabbed her ass.

"You didn't answer me, Elivia Noel." Calling her by full name to tell her I mean business. She swallowed hard, then smiled, "Yes, I'd love to be your girl!"

Then the lights turned back on. I got my girl and electricity. She hops up to turn up the heat. "Just in case it goes out again, cause brrrrrr! It is a bit chilly." She makes sure the fire is good and just as I'm about to move, "What are you doing? I got it handled; you rest."

"That's all I've been doing for two weeks straight. I'm not completely useless. Anyway, I was going to the bathroom."

"Oh, alright."

"Unless you want to hold my dick for me, can't say it won't be difficult to put back after you touch it, and I may take you in that closet of a bathroom. We've christened two rooms already. God help you when I get you in the shower..." I trailed off. I flipped the light switch and closed the door. I heard the stairs squeak, thinking she ran upstairs and did the same. When I came out, I checked the time on our phones; it was 48 minutes past midnight. I could see her smile from here as she stared at the snow that was at least a foot deep.

"It's exactly what I wanted! I hope we get at least five more feet, or it covers the entire house!"

"Whoa, that's a lot of snow, sweetheart. Even with this amount, we're not going anywhere. Let's not go crazy."

She smiles as she turns on some music and starts bouncing around like a kid hopped up on candy. It's funny how she still found Christmas music and that it's almost 1 a.m. and she took a nap at best and me...I yawn, and she stops, slapping her hands over her mouth.

"Oh my gosh, you haven't slept yet. I forgot. I'm so sorry, let's go to bed. You're still healing."

I pulled her against me, "Don't worry, I enjoyed your little show, but I have to admit I am tired after making you scream my name." I smile, and she rolls her eyes. She leads me to bed, and we get me settled first before she turns the lights off and lays beside me.

"You don't want any music playing?"

"No, I like the sound of the fireplace. Now go to sleep."

"I'll let that slide this time. Goodnight, Livi."

"Goodnight, Nicky." One last jab before we fall asleep in each other's arms or arm, in my case.

The light of the morning woke me from my slumber. Was it all a dream from the drugs prescribed because I was on some pretty powerful shit? I looked over to see that it was real; last night was real.

She was sleeping facing away from me and curled up in the blankets, burrowed deep. I noticed the fire was about out and we lost power again. It takes me a few tries, but I'm up and moving the ash away from the center and placing new logs on. I get a good roar going and the heat radiates the space fast.

I assessed the situation outside; the snowfall was light, and it looked like about three feet had fallen. I turn on the television with the volume on low.

"Officially, the average totals are between 20 inches in the low-lying areas and up to 52 inches in the mountains. Now focusing on local areas, Princeton received 42 inches, with Hermann receiving the least at only 24 inches, a vast difference when they are only ten miles apart. Culver received 48 inches and Asher Falls 39 inches. Power has been intermittent, and crews have been dispatched..." I turned the volume down.

　　She was still sleeping peacefully and while watching her, I realized I was looking at my girlfriend.

　　She was officially mine and I hadn't felt this happy in a long time. All I knew these past years was the darkness of loss, heartbreak, pity, and deep-seated anger. I'd like to think my mom waited for the right time to send her to me. Now, instead of dwelling on the past, I can start my own future.

26

ELIVIA

A *few weeks later*

IT'S BEEN an interesting few weeks. After making it official while snowed in, we spent New Year's the same way but only with a light coat of snow. Our first kiss of the new year consisted of party hats, favors, and nothing else.

Nick was able to start rehab. They picked him up from his house in the wee early hour of 6 a.m. I offered to drive him, but he said it was unnecessary and he would tie me to the bed and leave me if I offered again. I could see the advantages and disadvantages of that threat.

Anyway, they usually drop him off around noon and we would find something to do around town. Yesterday, he took me to the pizzeria that Xavier brought to me at work, but I didn't mention it. Once I was stuffed with delicious artisan pizza, I convinced him to come to the shop with me.

"Baby, I'm sure Angel has the shop covered. She's going to

yell at you much like I am." I pulled him in, and the bell rang. Angel definitely gave me the 'What are you doing here' look, but I held my hand up.

"Before you start, I'm not here as an employee." I looked back and he was doing the stretching exercises they told him to do when he felt tight. "I'm here as a customer. I know the Valentine's Day shipment came in and I placed an order to ship with it."

"Oh yeah, I saw a package with your name. I should have known. It's in the back, follow me."

"Hon, I'll be right back." He nods and looks around the store.

Angellica hands me a pink box in the office. "Thank you! Nick will be pleasantly surprised." I laugh, but Angel doesn't. "What's wrong?"

She looked around, closed her eyes, and then sighed hard, "I don't want you to worry, but Xavier came into the shop the day we opened from the holidays. I told him you were unavailable for an extended amount of time. He left without incident, but he seems to be walking by the store more than before. He's looking for you."

She seemed worried, but I was irritated. "I would think it would be common knowledge that Nick and I are together, but I guess not. Just stick with your story and eventually, he'll stop. Call Colby if you feel uncomfortable."

"I will."

Like Nick and I, Angel and Colby are in a blossoming relationship. Seeing them together still makes my heart flutter. Seems he's been keeping her company when his shift ends while she's at work. She always sends him home to rest, but he won't go unless she promises to come by after she is off. They're growing comfortable enough to hang out at each other's place.

I try to change to a more positive subject, "Have you heard from the mama-to-be?"

"Kelly? Yeah, she called me in tears when Beck refused to get her apples and cheddar cheese to go with her vegetable soup. He eventually went when she said that he didn't love her or the baby. When the door closed, she stopped and giggled, saying this is what she has to resort to now. I guess we should all get together since we haven't seen each other since Christmas."

"Sure, let's schedule it for Saturday at Nick's place." We walk back out, and Nick is touching the Sexy Sweetheart set that consists of a pink teddy and matching fingerless gloves. I cleared my throat, and he jumped back. "I, uh, was just looking."

"Looks like more than looking..." He looked kind of embarrassed that Angel and I both caught him. I laugh as I walk toward him. I grab his hand, "I already have that set at home... in two colors. Guess there'll be no doubt what to wear tonight. See you Saturday, Angel!"

A few days later, I was at the store because Angellica had an appointment, and I was bored at home while Nick was in rehab. He was getting his cast off, and they'll assess if he needs any type of brace afterward.

I was catching up on sending reports to headquarters and sending the next inventory order. I missed this and even though it was temporary, and I'll be resuming my duties soon, I'm glad to be at work. The smiles of the women and men, I think everyone was getting used to buying regularly here. I even started greeting people by name. I finally met Olivia Jones, the lady with seven kids. She was drop-dead gorgeous and didn't even look like she had one child. She and her husband roamed around the store, talking, and picking up items. I noticed her pick up the Love Me Tender Teddy, the Celestial nightgown, and they picked up the Sexy Secrets board game. I see why they have so many kids; they keep their relationship fun and fresh.

"Here you go, Olivia. I hope you and John enjoy."

"Oh, we will. Bye, Elivia!" I wave as the bell signals their exit, but immediately rings again.

"Welcome to Sugar Sweet. How can I help you?" I look up to see Xavier at the door. His stance and energy make me uncomfortable. "If you aren't buying anything, you can leave. We have nothing to talk about."

He smiles as he approaches the counter, "*Mi Amor*, we have much to discuss. Especially after you kicked me in the balls, that wasn't nice, and I think you owe me. How about you cook me dinner to say you're sorry?" There was a sinisterness to how calm he was. I was not comfortable in his presence, but I wouldn't show it. I dug down deep. "You're delusional. Nick and I are together, end of conversation."

"Come on, how much longer are you going to babysit the mama's boy? You know that you and I make more sense than you and him. Let me prove it to you in every way."

"What part of no don't you understand?" I was starting to get annoyed. I kept looking at the door, hoping someone would come in. Fate was not on my side and my uneasiness increased.

He leaned forward and grazed my cheek, "I'll get you and my apology soon enough. You might say no now, but you know you want me. From the first moment you walked into the cafe. The connection was immediate, and I could have sealed the deal after the town festival if you hadn't run off to be with him."

"My mind was set then, and it is now. Nothing's changed; I don't know how many times I need to say it."

"You keep telling yourself that you'll be mine eventually. One way...or another..."

What does that mean? I know it wasn't good because my stomach dropped and suddenly, I wanted to be as far away from him as possible, but he made the first move, heading toward the door.

"I will see you soon, Elivia. I'm in your head now." He laughed as he left. I suddenly felt nauseous, and I don't feel safe here. I decided to close up early and go home. I had a dilemma of whether or not to tell Nick what happened.

Xavier was more bark than bite, or at least that's what I was trying to convince myself. I felt so much relief after parking and walking over to his place. Nick and I exchanged keys about two weeks ago and we would alternate between places. When I walked in, he looked pleasantly surprised to see me.

"Hey babe, you're off early." I don't know why I felt so emotional, but my throat tightened, and the tears formed. I wasn't going to say anything, but now I have to explain why I was shaking and crying in his arms.

He pulled me away and put his hands on my face, which I realized, "Your cast is off. Does it hurt?"

"Don't change the subject. What happened?"

"It's nothing. I thought this situation was over, but I was wrong...when Xavier came into the shop."

"What?!" He was immediately pissed. I could see the rage behind his eyes. "I'm going to kill that son of a bitch! What happened, tell me every detail, Livi. Don't try to sugarcoat it."

He was right. It was serious. I thought the situation was dead and buried, but it had been simmering in a pot until he could confront me. We sat down on the couch, and I spilled all the details, including his open-ended vow to see me again.

"You're staying here tonight. Beck and I are going to have some words with Xavier. And don't try to calm me down and tell me not to. I'm going to knock his teeth down his throat for threatening you!"

"It wasn't a threat." I was trying to do exactly what he told me not to do: calm him down.

He looked at me with so much anger, "Elivia, I dropped this when you told me to. He was no longer a factor once you made the decision to pick me over him and I was grateful to have such a beautiful girl at my side. My job is to protect you and I'll be damned if I let this slide. I'm going to end it, period."

He started pacing after saying his final word and all I could do was watch. I had to voice my concern, "I–I don't want you to get hurt again. It's bad enough that what you do is dangerous, but to risk injury or worse over someone who doesn't matter? It's not worth it."

That took the wind out of his sails, and he sat back down, contemplating. "Being a firefighter's girlfriend isn't easy and I get it. I'll just talk and threaten to separate his spine from his body if he approaches you again. Better? Only words."

"Only words, no actions?"

He kissed me, "No violence, unless provoked, then all bets are off."

"That's fair."

"Let me call Beck and give him the details. I'll be back." He pulled his phone from his pocket and walked to the back, and I heard the back door open.

Well, that didn't go as I planned, but I did feel better. I went into the kitchen to see he had tried to start dinner; his mobility was still limited, judging by the rough nature of the chopped peppers. I chopped them even smaller, along with the onion that was still whole. Judging by the ingredients, he was making fajitas. By the time the door opened, I had finished cooking the steak strips and put the peppers and onion back into the pan.

I was reaching for the plates when he wrapped his arms around me, his newly freed arm significantly looser than the other. I let go of the plates to avoid dropping them. Then he sat me on the island. I leaned down for a kiss. "Thank you, you didn't have to cook. I was going to surprise you after a hard day at work, especially after you spent all this time taking care of me. Thank you for being there."

"Anything for you. Now, what did Beck say?"

"He said I have every right to bash his head in if he approaches you again. No, he said he was going to give a heads-up to a friend of ours in the police department to start a paper trail."

"A paper trail is good; it'll keep you out of prison." I laughed, but I was serious. Xavier wasn't worth it; he wasn't worth the attention he got from us today. I just wanted to live in our bubble in peace.

"Let's eat!"

The next morning, we walked over to my place so I could change. Today was going to be a chill day for both of us. One thing he said was right; he was in my head. I didn't feel safe at work by myself and even with Angellica there, I'd worry about both of us. I was starting to live in fear. Nick was already at rehab when I brewed myself some coffee and popped a bagel in the toaster.

I was thinking about the next holiday, which was Valentine's Day. I used to be so anti-Valentine's because I never felt special. Most guys bought something out of obligation. Nothing came from the heart. They expected sex after their thoughtless cheap baubles like a stuffed animal and chocolate were supposed to wow me enough to rip off my clothes; little did they know I had a garbage bag full of these gifts that I donated to a children's hospital before I left. I wanted our first Valentine's Day to be special, from his end and mine. I was on my computer researching ideas when I heard the door handle jiggle. For a split second, I was terrified until I saw his smile.

He set his gym bag down. "Hey, darlin'."

"Hey, how was rehab?"

"Good, another week or so and I'll be clear to start training with the guys. I miss those bastards."

"I know they miss you, too. Soon, everything will be back to normal."

My cell started ringing, but it was on the counter in the kitchen. It eventually stopped as he lay in my lap. Then my phone rang again. "You should get that."

I groan and go to answer my phone, "Hello."

"Livi! They screwed up the order and they won't fix it because I didn't place the order. They need you."

"Can they do it over the phone?" I whine, trying not to leave the comfort of my house.

"No, they need you to confirm what was supposed to be ordered and sign the amended order slip. It's madness! And I have customers. They're threatening to leave the bad shipment here!" She was panicking, but it was no problem; it was a quick fix.

"Okay, alright, I'm coming, don't worry, I'll be there in five minutes."

I groan loudly. "Hey baby, sorry, Angel is freaking out over an error in our shipment. I have to go fix it, but I'll be back. I made pasta salad and it's in the fridge."

"Okay, I'll be here when you return."

I grab my keys and open the door, "Nick, you're blocking me in. Honey…"

He grabbed me and kissed me. I almost wanted to stay, then he held up his keys. "Take mine."

"Are you going to help me get into it? I almost drove into the ditch last time."

"You need to get used to it like I have to with your fancy wheels."

I sigh and take them. "I'm not responsible for any damage." With a literal running start, I was in it and on my way to the shop.

27

NICK

S he didn't want to go in and I know it's because of Xavier. She shouldn't have to live in fear of some loser with a chip on his shoulder. Beck reminded me of what Chief said, to stay away from the cafe and that's okay, I'd catch him elsewhere. He was casing the store and that would be my best bet in catching him.

But first, I need a shower. I was stiff and sore. I head up to her room, slip off everything in the bedroom, and walk into her bathroom. It was a pretty decent size shower, definitely larger than standard showers. I turned on the water and looked in the mirror. I was growing a goatee, and she joked that by next Christmas, I could have an actual Santa beard and I could dye it for the season. It's a thought to really immerse myself. Speaking of Christmas, I was planning something very special to celebrate us, the season, and possibly entering the contest together.

The steam was an indicator that it was the right temperature and I stepped in, coming face to face with my enemy, Tony. I picked him up this time, analyzing him and scoffing at this pink device. "What's so special about you? I can make her cum too." I saw the buttons on the side of the handle and began pressing. It went from silent to buzzing to shaking and buzzing, doing its best to hit all the spots. Then there were levels to the vibrations from sweet and smooth to absolutely rocking the walls. I stop it and stare, "Well played, sir. Perhaps we can work together for our common goal."

I put him back and lather up, letting the hot water massage the soreness away and start daydreaming about Livi coming back, catching me in the shower, and joining me.

I heard a creak and thought she was back from her work emergency and coming up the stairs. I grab a towel to wrap around myself and a smaller one to wipe my face. I contemplate whether or not to come down as is, to surprise her with a romp on the kitchen counter again. We have christened almost every room minus the half bath and though tricky, I am still determined. Hmm, why not now? It'll take her mind off of work. I spray on my cologne and step out. I decided to wear my boxers because there was a chance that Angellica could be with her after that fiasco and that would be awkward if I came down in only a towel trying to flash my girlfriend. Better safe than sorry.

As I walk down the stairs, I see a figure walk out the side kitchen door, but she leaves it open.

Maybe she's taking out the garbage because it stinks in here.

I thought, but it wasn't a normal smell. I followed to the door and looked down after I stepped in something liquid. I crouch down and sniff it...

It smells like...

I see a trail from the kitchen that leads outside. I walk toward the door and peek outside to see...

"HEY, YOU SON OF A BITCH!"

That's all I remember, and then I blacked out.

～

Elivia

"Seriously, she's my manager. This could have been done through her. Next time, you know."

"Sorry, ma'am. It's company protocol, but we will make a note for future deliveries and apologize to you. It won't happen again." He says to Angellica.

"It's fine." Which means she wasn't fine, but she was keeping it professional. The bell signaled their exit.

"Are you okay?" I ask while she checks out a customer.

"It's because I look like a child! No one takes me seriously. I'm fine; there's nothing you can do about it. Thanks for coming by."

"No problem. The day is almost over. Why don't you wrap up these people in line, then we'll grab stuff for a taco/nacho night and invite the gang? Sound good?"

"Yeah," She said sadly. I hug her and start closing procedures while she does checkout.

I know he isn't cleared for work, but my ears are keen to the sirens approaching then passing by; it was accompanied by an ambulance.

Hmm, it seems serious, whatever it was.

Since the shipment was incorrect, we couldn't set it up for Valentine's Day. The corrected one should be here in a few days. I started prepping one of the areas.

"So, how are you and Colby?" I tried to talk about something that made her smile, and he always made her smile. She was grinning from ear to ear when she heard his name, "Oh my gosh, he is so wonderful! He's planning a night under the stars soon. He's looking for the best spot for stargazing and camping."

"That sounds so cool and romantic."

"What about you and Nick?"

"We're so comfortable now, like an old married couple. We alternate between our houses."

"Do you think you'll move into one house or the other permanently?"

That was a good question. I guess I was too wrapped up in bliss to wonder what the next big step would be.

We were startled by banging and I saw Kelly knocking frantically on the door. Maybe she had to pee; she was holding her belly. I walked as quickly to unlock the door, "Is the baby kicking mommy's bladder? Bathroom is in the..."

"No! Livi, your house is on fire!"

"MY WHAT?!"

"Beck called from the firehouse when it came in."

Then I thought about it. "Oh God, Nick's at my house. I have to go!" I think they said they'd follow me. I wasn't listening. I had to get home.

I started to see gray smoke around my neighborhood, and then I saw the fire truck, the ambulance and now three cop cars were all parked around my house. I didn't see any flames. I guess that was good. Judging by the unrolled hose, they put it out, but how much damage was done?

I park his truck and hop out. Trying to look for him, why else would the ambulance be here?

"Nick! Nick!" I finally get past all the vehicles and see Nick sitting on my porch...in handcuffs. Beck was there to intercept.

"Nick!" Beck stops me and I shove him off.

"Livi, listen to me. Please." He tried to get me to look at him by getting in my line of sight. "I need to tell you what happened."

"Why can't he tell me? He's right there." I beg; I can feel the tears as I run my fingers through my hair.

"He's in custody. He needs a lawyer for what he did. I advised him not to say anything. In reality, I think he's in shock. He hasn't said much of anything."

It didn't make sense; I needed the whole story. He was in his boxers, in handcuffs and only looking at the ground. But something was off with him.

"What happened?"

"Apparently, he caught Xavier trying to set your place on fire. He poured gas from the kitchen to the outside; he was going to lock you in and set it on fire. He didn't know Nick was here. Nick caught him as he lit the outside. And with all the conflict between them, he...well, he beat him unconscious. He's being charged with aggravated battery. It's serious, but I got a friend who's a lawyer on his way to the precinct. He's going to jail, Livi, at least for tonight."

I can't believe what is happening! "He was going to kill me?! Because I wouldn't go out with him, that I picked Nick over him?! That son of a bitch deserved whatever he got!"

Nick still wouldn't look at me. "What's wrong with him?"

"He said he doesn't remember what happened, he blacked out in rage and thought you would be disappointed." I went around Beck and knelt down on the ground. He looked like he took a few licks, but his hands indicated more was dealt than taken. I was more worried about his healing arm. I pulled his chin up and he finally looked at me, "I'm sorry."

"What? No, don't ever apologize. I'm not mad or disappointed. Listen to me. You protected me like you said you would, and I love you for it."

His face lit up, "You love me?" I let the tears fall as I realized I said it. "Yes, Nicky, I love you and we are going to fight this. I'll always be there, okay?"

"Okay."

An officer approached, "Miss Winters, can you come inside and answer a few questions?"

"Sure." I follow him in and immediately smell gas. It's all over my kitchen and living room floor to the outside. He walks me through areas they already gathered for evidence, and we end the questioning looking at the charred part of the outside of my house. It wasn't a lot of damage, but it was noticeable. I told the officer my side, from the time I moved here to his threatening pre-arson visit at the shop. I asked to press arson and endangerment charges against him.

"Depending on if he makes it through the night, ma'am. He roughed him up good. He might not make it."

"I hope you don't expect me to feel sorry for a man who was willing to set me on fire because I rejected him because I don't."

"Livi!" I hear Beck call me and I rush back around to the front. "They're going to take him in and charge him."

"But he's naked."

"I'll grab some clothes and head down there. Pack a bag. You're going to stay with Kels and me per his request."

"Can I see him before they put him in the car?"

"Yeah, not for long."

He was standing and had an officer next to him. "Nick..." My words caught in my throat and the tears formed. I looked away.

"Hey, I'm okay, it'll be okay. I don't regret anything as long as you are safe. I love you, Elivia."

"I-I love you too, Nick. I'll be okay." I nod to keep from bawling. I felt hands on my arm; it was Kelly. "Come on, let's pack some clothes and supplies."

They put Nick in the squad car and drove away.

What is happening in my life?

The night went by quickly, I barely ate and wanted to sleep my troubles away. I can imagine the town gossip from this. No matter what they say, he was a hero. My hero, they were not going to make him the bad guy.

The next morning, I lay in the guest bedroom looking at the ceiling. Nick was facing serious charges, and I had to clean and repair my house. I wanted no trace of it ever happening.

All of this was so overwhelming it was late in the morning

and I hadn't even gotten out of bed. I wasn't hungry, I didn't want to talk, I felt super emotional. I only wanted to be held by Nick.

Knock knock

"Go away, I don't need or want anything. Leave me alone." I didn't want to sound mean, but my heart was hurting. I heard the door open anyway. "Livi." I turn to see Nick and I immediately hug him. "They let you out?"

"Yeah, with my testimony, yours and now Beck's, Angel's, and a few people from the firehouse, they're trying to go for self-defense and charge him with first-degree felony arson since I was in the house and attempted second-degree murder. Either way, if he's convicted, he's out of our lives for good."

"I'm so angry! He could have killed you!"

"Me? He was trying to kill you! He didn't realize that you took my car instead of yours. He thought you were home upstairs in the shower, but it was me. What if he tried to assault you instead of..." He had to pause to calm his anger, "When I came down, I stepped in the gasoline, I knew that smell anywhere and when I saw him trying to light the side of the house, a switch flipped."

"Do you really not remember?"

"Only bits and pieces are coming back, but mostly no. Hopefully, it does return by the time the trial comes around."

"Trial?"

"Yeah, the bastard survived. I might still get charged for assault if the self-defense plea doesn't work out."

I hugged him. I didn't care; he was here with me now.

"Kiss me." He didn't hesitate, laying me down and covering my body with his.

"Mmmm..."

I wanted to forget what happened these past 24 hours, except that we confessed our love to each other.

"Wait!" I push him away and he looks at me, "We are not at home; they'll hear us!"

"No, they won't."

"Yes, we will! Don't you dare think about defiling our guest bedroom, you two. In fact, come on and eat, both of you."

He follows me out to face a very irritated Kelly. I rub her belly, "Yes, mom."

I felt better and my appetite was returning. Nick pulled me as close as he could without actually sitting me on his lap.

I gasped, "Oh no, your rehab! We missed today's session."

"Beck called them, and I got released to return to the station and train with them. They said I was a week ahead of schedule anyway."

"Chief is going to run you through the ringer for going against his orders."

"But I didn't; that asshole came looking for trouble and he got it."

"I'll say. Three broken ribs, two black eyes, a broken nose and jaw, internal bleeding and swelling."

"Hey, he got a few shots in. This black eye didn't just appear and I'm sore and bruised all over from the body shots. Now we wait on formal charges for both of us."

I squeeze his hand and we look at each for a moment.

"Oh, good grief, they're doing it again. I feel my breakfast coming back up from this sugary sweet moment."

"Shut up!"

He places his hand on my chin, "Pay her no mind. She can't keep me down after you told me you love me."

"OH MY GOD, LIVI! You did what?!" Kelly leaned back against the counter, rubbing her stomach with her smile a mile wide.

"I told Nick I loved him, and he said he loved me too. Minus the circumstances, it was a perfect moment."

Beep beep, beep beep

Both of them checked their pagers.

"Uhh, we got to go, meeting at the firehouse. My lawyer is going to be there to gather evidence. Stay here, and after, we'll go to my place."

"I need to clean the house and air it out."

"Absolutely not; it needs proper disposal. Kelly, call Daisy Mae, she owns a cleaning service, and her husband does junk removal. You'll need to clear out everything in the living room and we may need to replace the flooring depending on the damage. You'll stay with me in the meantime. Go pack and I'll meet you after this meeting. Okay?"

I lean super close to his ear, whispering, "Yes, Santa." His eyes light up and with no other words, they leave for the firehouse.

28

NICK

Four *months later:*
It's been an interesting time; I have resumed my training while preparing for trial on the charges against me. I felt not an inkling of remorse and honestly, I only remember bits and pieces still, but judging by what Colby witnessed in the hospital, I nearly beat him to death. He was going to burn her alive in her own home!

We had the flooring redone, and the furniture replaced. She has spent more time at my place due to the trauma, but occasionally, I convince her to stay there and remind her how cozy it is and that she is safe.

She has resumed working her normal hours at the shop and preparing displays for the next holiday, Mother's Day, and I had something very special planned for that day.

That morning, I told her to wear something nice and she chose a vibrant yellow floral dress and a straw hat. I handed her a bouquet of daisies. "But you already gave me flowers."

"I know, these aren't for you. Hold them, please." I hold her hand as we pull into the parking lot and help her down. She adjusts herself and makes sure everything is in place and that she looks perfect for this moment. She grabs the flowers, "Okay, I think I'm ready." I grab the blanket and basket and she follows me until I stop.

My throat swells: it's been a while since I visited, and I never brought anyone. I could feel myself choking back the tears as I laid down the blanket and basket and stood back up, "Mom, Dad, this is Elivia. She's been taking care of me now. She's...my girlfriend."

She smiles as she kneels down on the blanket, "It's so nice to meet you. We brought you flowers for Mother's Day, Mrs. Nicholas. Happy Mother's Day. I hope you get to meet my dad in Heaven. The three of you could watch over us and tell stories about us as kids. He would love to know someone like you, I think."

She paused for a moment to look away; we'll have to do something special for her father on Father's Day.

"I'm thankful for you and the son you raised. He makes me happy." She placed the flowers on her grave, and I put a nice cigar on my father's grave. I pull her against me and bask in the breeze and a perfect sunny day.

"Thank you for being here. I've never brought anyone out here with me."

She nodded and we basked in the beauty of this day and moment before the sunset.

The following month was the hearing to see what charges Xavier was being charged with. Elivia didn't want to go, but I convinced her to show him she was safe and didn't fear him.

It didn't last long; the formal hearing was set for some time in September, and they denied his bail. He would have to rot in there until then.

As for me, because of his injuries and his charges, I was charged with a Class A assault charge, fined $4000 and put on one year's probation instead of jail time. My long-standing within the community and testimonies from my boss and my workmates helped my case. I joke to Livi that she's dating a bad boy now; she just rolls her eyes.

Elivia

My 'convict' boyfriend loves to remind me that he did time, all 16 hours and that he didn't know if he could play Santa this year for the town now that he had a rap sheet and street cred. He said he might rock a sleeveless suit with tattoos and a cigar.

I dealt with this from sentencing through the summer and most of the fall. I let him think what he wants. I'm glad he wasn't severely punished for his actions. He was my hero.

Xavier was sentenced to ten years in prison, with a minimum of seven years to complete before he could be eligible for parole. He had a permanent restraining order and could never step foot in Asher Falls again. I don't think I'll ever feel 100% safe, but I'll deal with that when we're notified of his hearing.

After Halloween and Thanksgiving, we were now in our season. The season I met the most wonderful man. He had started planning since Halloween but wouldn't reveal it until after Thanksgiving. Immediately after Thanksgiving, he started tearing up a piece of land on the opposite side of his house where I couldn't see. For the next week, whenever he wasn't on duty, he was working on it. He said he needed it completed before we started decorating for the competition.

Last weekend was when he got most of the work done. I heard the sounds of clanging, banging, and power tools. I could simply walk over but promised him I would wait until he was finished. Because of his secret project, I wasn't allowed in his house either. It was okay, I had started to feel at home in my place after the incident, and the new flooring, now with heating elements, made the frigid nights better. I didn't have to wear heavy socks. I lounge on my new emerald-green sofa and find the first of many Hallmark movies to come. My romantic moment butterflies were fluttering. They all have the same premise with only slight changes.

It was me and my popcorn until I fell asleep.

"Come on, baby. To bed...I don't know if you can hear me, but I finished it and tomorrow night, I'll reveal it."

29

NICK

Tonight was the culmination of hard work and almost an entire year together. I made her promise not to come snooping over at my house until the project was complete. As much as I would love to rely on Mother Nature for snow, I couldn't risk it and had a backup plan.

And although we'd been together all this time, I had yet to give her this. I started my shift tomorrow, so it had to be tonight.

I cooked dinner at her place and then instructed her to dress warmly. She came back down, and I had her winter coat ready; there was no snow, but it was close to freezing temps outside. She bundled up and took my hand and I led her outside and over to my place.

I walked over to the other side of the house, and she gasped. "Oh my God..." I pressed the button of the remote in my pocket and the area was filling with light snowflakes from the machine.

She stood in awe of the new gazebo in my yard. Strewn with fairy lights and now covered in snow. I bring her under the gazebo and take her hand.

"Ever since you told Santa what you wanted for Christmas; I've been trying to find an opportunity to fulfill it. Elivia, you have been my saving grace since my parent's death. You made me mad; you made me laugh, and you made me realize life wasn't so bad. You are the type of woman my mother would love to call her daughter-in-law. She would have loved you, and I knew I couldn't spend another holiday without giving you that holiday romance kiss under the gazebo...after I ask you to marry me."

She gasped and covered her mouth, "Elivia Noel Winters, will you marry me and enter the competition as a team? Mr. and Mrs. Claus...for life."

I kneel and present the ring in the box. She chuckles, knowing she would have to deal with this kink of mine for life.

"Oh, St. Nick! Of course, I will!" I slip the ring on, lift her up, and kiss her as the snow falls around us. Eventually, I put her down and wiped the tears away.

"Ahhh! I can't believe it! It's my perfect Hallmark moment with the best guy ever. You built this...for me..."

"I did. I dreamed of this moment with you since you left me with a hard-on at the shopping center, telling Santa you'd be daddy's good girl."

She gives me a mischievous smile, "I did, and I am. So, what about the competition this year? How are we going to work together with two houses?"

"We're going to enter your place, and my house will be an extension of yours, like a bonus."

"But you're the reigning champion. Don't you want to defend your title?"

I look around the neighborhood; some houses are starting to prep, but then I look at the gift in my arms and smile.

"I got what I wanted for Christmas, but if you win, it'll be the start of a new tradition between the two of us."

She pulled me down for another steamy kiss.

"I'm pretty sure you mean between the...three of us."

Merry Christmas!

EPILOGUE

NICK

One Year Later

"Anyone want to cover for me tomorrow?" Perry asked the group. Everyone kept putting their equipment away.

"What for?" Jackson shouted. I could hear the annoyance in his voice.

He looked around and then sighed, "I forgot to buy my wife this perfume set, and it's sold out here. Now I have to drive all the way to Pittsburgh to pick up an order." A chorus of groans rang out. We all knew.

"Still making rookie mistakes?! I'll cover, but you owe me." Lewis, the new guy, says. He transferred over from Hermann company. We met him after that granary accident. The whole company came to visit the firehouse and even me in the hospital. He was a single guy, actually, he was the new me. He was hopeful to start fresh here in Asher Falls. He was a good guy and an even more awesome firefighter.

"Nick, are we still having dinner at your house?" Beck shuts his locker and gathers his laundry bag.

"Yeah, her parents are going to have dinner at the Italian place tonight and watch the sunset at the park. You know cute couple stuff. Elivia has been so happy since they came and visited her here. She got to meet my parents and now I have met hers and, of course, they love me." Beck rolls his eyes, throwing his bag over his shoulder. He waves at me. "Oh and bring the presents so we can exchange them. I know my little buddy is going to love what Uncle Nick got him."

Beck sighed, "Is it something noisy and torturous to his parent's ears? You do know that now we can return the favor. He may not be able to play with them right now, but eventually, he'll have a nice shiny drum set like Uncle Nick bought his nephew."

"It's a perfect time!"

"He's only one and a half, Uncle Nick. He just started saying other words besides mama and dada; I don't think he's ready for a drum solo. You're making me second guess you as a godparent." He laughs. I know he doesn't mean it. I'm spoiling him because he was my test child before I had my own. He's my little guy.

I lift my bag, "See you in an hour or so? I'm sure Livi's already cooking up a storm." He nods and we're all on our way home.

I pull my truck into the driveway next to her car and our more appropriate sedan we use for family outings. I still smile when I see the car seat.

We had just completed the design and execution of our holiday entry. Our theme was, 'Santa Clause, me, and baby makes three,' playing up on our newest addition to the Nicholas family. Even though we had completely moved into my house, we extended our display to her home too. She brought up selling it, but I convinced her we could use the space to relax, take a break from reality, or be a quiet place to concentrate on some project. Besides, it was there we shared our most memorable moments and a few not-so-happy ones. I think she's still traumatized seeing me handcuffed and the side of her house charred.

"Honey?"

"In the kitchen!"

I set my stuff down, turn on our display, and walk back.

I see her at the stove, stirring a big pot with him in the baby wrap and her free hand cradling him. She kisses the top of his head, and he coos. I still can't believe that we were parents to this precious baby boy.

She had picked the perfect name for him, combining my work and our extended family to name him Asher Tyler Nicolas, or Ash for short. Of course, we made Kelly and Tyler godparents, but they did not know that Livi had planned to give him Beck's name. Even though they had done the same to me when their son was born. When Decker was born, I found out when I saw his name on the birth card: Decker Nicholas Beckham.

"No way...you guys didn't..." I was speechless and could only hug them. Livi saw it and started crying profusely, blaming her hormones.

"Hey, how was work?" She leaned in for a kiss before putting the lid on the pot.

"Good, we were training the new guy on protocol. He's going to fit in just fine."

"We should invite him over for the main holiday dinner. He's single, right?"

"Yeah."

"Hmm, I have to see who I have available. I'm running out of single friends.

"Calm down, matchmaker, he just got here. Now, give me my little guy. I'm sure your back hurts from carrying him for so long. I know you haven't put him down since you started cooking. Where are your parents?" She looked guilty because she knew I was right. I slide him off his mom and he starts to fuss. "Hey, it's daddy-son time now." His eyes open to see me and he gives me a smile. "Hey, daddy's big boy." I hear her sigh in relief. I knew she wouldn't say it, but she needed to rest her back.

"They went to the restaurant a little early because they're going to do a picnic at the park. I gave them my basket and wine set for ambiance. They almost took Asher with them, but I told them that Decker would be here, and it would be awkward with just one child by himself. He needs his play buddy."

That's fair, they are more like cousins and get so active when they are around each other.

She kissed my cheek, "I'm going to shower and change before everyone gets here. He already ate and he's either going to poop or sleep. Possibly both."

"Daddy can handle that, can't he? Ash and I are fine."

Elivia

SOMEHOW, this shower felt magical. Maybe because I had been in the kitchen since noon, preparing this meal for the family. Mom and dad had taken Asher most of the day and eventually, I whined to get my baby boy back. What can I say, I love my new role as a mother, but he was wreaking havoc on my back.

But I couldn't be happier. This was what I had always hoped for: small-town living with a beautiful home, fiancé, and that adorable little bundle of joy down there.

Asher and Nick were the perfect additions to my life, and I wouldn't change anything, even those series of unfortunate events, because without those, who knows how our story would have turned out.

I dressed and went into Ash's room to grab his clothes, but they weren't there. I came back down to see if Nick had seen them. "Nick, have you seen Ash's holiday outfit? It was his little elf one..." I was pleasantly surprised to see he was already dressed, and his bib was covering it in an attempt to keep it clean long enough for me to get a photo.

"Aww, look at my munchkin, he's so cute! Picture time for mommy while daddy takes a shower." It wasn't an ask; he smelled like soot, and he didn't say a word as he handed him over and went upstairs.

I was able to take five pictures before he threw up all over and the bib caught most and only his collar was soaked.

"You gave me enough photos, but now we have to find another bib, Ashy!"

"Please don't call my son that; it's bad enough everyone calls me Nicky now. Don't torture my boy."

He came down in a simple white button-down and blue slacks. He always looked so hot when he dressed up.

"It's just a nickname. I promise it won't leave the house. Let me check the food before they arrive."

I hand him over, but he pulls me back for a steamy kiss. One filled with passion and intent. Lucky for him, I have quite the holiday surprise. Sugar Sweet is going to launch a lingerie line that I helped put together and I had all the outfits before next week's launch. He would get a sneak peek preview tonight.

"Did I tell you how beautiful you look?"

I hold my arms out in front, accentuating my breasts in my dress. "No, Santa."

"It's not going to be a silent night tonight."

I groan at how corny he's getting. It's getting worse, but then I laugh because he knows it's bad.

"Hey! We're here!" Kelly comes in with a crockpot in one

hand and Decker trying to keep up in the other. Beck follows with his arms full of boxes and before the door closes, Colby and Angellica come in with food and gifts.

"Put the gifts under the tree, everyone. Decker are you going to walk to me?! Already? It's too soon!" He giggles with his arms out for uppies, and I couldn't resist those rosy cheeks. He was the spitting image of his daddy. Same for Ash; it's like Kelly and I were just ovens for their twins.

A bit later, after dinner, we're all sat by the huge tree exchanging gifts. Colby and Angel gifted each couple with a weekend at a scenic Airbnb and offered to babysit. They said it would be good practice for when they have kids.

Kelly and Beck's was a mountain retreat and Nick and I to a themed cabin near Morgantown. "Santa's Secret Village?" I perused the brochure. It was an adult playland for Christmas lovers. I didn't even look in his direction to know he was smiling like a raving lunatic. "Thanks for playing into his kink; now he'll make this a yearly thing."

"You bet your sweet ass I will, Mrs. Claus."

I ignore him and slide a big box over, "For my handsome Decker."

"God help you, Nick if it's a drum set!" Beck warns; he pops the top and Decker squeals. He pulls out a fire engine and fireman costume for him.

Kelly gasps, "It's so cute! Thank you Auntie Livi and Uncle Nick!" Beck looked relieved; he had been uneasy since the floor keyboard Nick bought him for his birthday. He loves that keyboard, and they hope the batteries wear out. I hand them an envelope. Kels opens it, "Oh, free massages at that new spa! We definitely need this."

She hugs me, "And you know we'll watch our favorite little guy." She nods, handing Beck the envelope and brochure.

"Oh, I have one more surprise for my girls and an

announcement. No, I'm not pregnant." Everyone seemed to exhale at once.

"I have been secretly collaborating with Sugar Sweet on a line of lingerie centered around the holidays, and I secured some Christmas treats for the ladies to showcase at home. It's from the Mr. & Mrs. Claus line, naturally. So, here you go."

Angellica immediately went red. Kels had no problem holding up the Racy Rudolph set and riding crop. It comes with a red "nose," but it's not a nose but a gag. Beck just looks at me and I shrug. He decides to take her attention by giving her his gift.

Nick cozies up behind me on the floor, "Tell me, Mrs. Claus, is there a box of holiday goodies for me to...unwrap. I much prefer unwrapping my gifts, as you know." He still knew how to rile me up.

"I'm sorry, Santa, I was a bad girl and didn't wrap them, but the entire collection is upstairs in my drawer. I'll let you pick what outfit I jingle your bells in."

He cringes, "Okay, that was terrible. Let's leave the sexy sayings to me."

Well, I tried.

"Oh! One more thing... we will all be taking a trip to NYC the day after tomorrow to see the Macy's display, skate at Rockefeller Square, and much more. So, go pack and be back here tomorrow night to leave bright and early Saturday morning at 5 a.m. Give me your top three places and I'll see how many we can complete."

"OMG! I'm so excited! Come on, Colby, let's go pack! Thank you!"

"We'll take your sedan and Beck's SUV, which should comfortably fit everyone. Come on, Decker, mommy's got to get you all packed up for your first big trip courtesy of Auntie Livi. Say bye-bye!" I drowned him in kisses, and she did the same to Ash.

Once everyone was gone and Ash was put to bed, I stood by the tree and was just gazing outside. No winter storm forecasted, but I was remembering when we were snowed in.

I felt his arms surround me, and he put down the baby monitor. Then he pulls my face in his direction, giving me a Christmas kiss that makes my knees buckle. Oh, what Santa does to me.

"Hey."

"Hey."

"Merry Christmas, Mrs. Claus."

"Merry Christmas, St. Nick."

THE END

Merry Christmas from Nick, Elivia & baby Asher!

FROM S COURTNEY

Thank you for taking the time to read Light the Way. I hope you enjoyed the book and would love if you could leave a review on any retailer or Goodreads.
If you would like to hear more from me about new releases and sales, follow me on:
Linktr.ee: https://linktr.ee/mskeiya
Website: https://scourtneybooks.com

www.ingramcontent.com/pod-product-compliance
Lightning Source LLC
Chambersburg PA
CBHW022042240626
47154CB00007B/2527